"You Want To Be Reckless And Irresponsible?"

"Yeah, totally yeah," Teague whispered.

Something warmed inside Daisy even more than all that hot, combustible sex. It was just…she hadn't planned on liking a man, really liking one, for at least another millennium. In fact, she liked him so much at that instant that she had to hesitate. "You don't think you're going to regret this? That we're moving too fast?"

"Of course we're going to regret this. Of course we're moving too fast." He was still aiming for another kiss, and his voice was thicker than honey. "You know damn well it never works out to have sex too soon. It takes over everything."

"I know. And I know better." She found herself staring at his mouth.

"So do I. Believe me, this is your call. Totally. You want to send up a stop sign, we quit, all's fair."

"What on earth made you think I was going to put up a stop sign?"

Dear Reader,

Welcome to another stellar month of smart, sensual reads. Our bestselling series DYNASTIES: THE DANFORTHS comes to a compelling conclusion with Leanne Banks's *Shocking the Senator* as honest Abe Danforth finally gets his story. Be sure to look for the start of our next family dynasty story when Eileen Wilks launches DYNASTIES: THE ASHTONS next month and brings you all the romance and intrigue you could ever desire…all set in the fabulous Napa Valley.

Award-winning author Jennifer Greene is back this month to conclude THE SCENT OF LAVENDER series with the astounding *Wild in the Moment*. And just as the year brings some things to a close, new excitement blossoms as Alexandra Sellers gives us the next installment of her SONS OF THE DESERT series with *The Ice Maiden's Sheikh*. The always-enjoyable Emilie Rose will wow you with her tale of *Forbidden Passion*—let's just say the book starts with a sexy tryst on a staircase. We'll let you imagine the rest. Brenda Jackson is also back this month with her unforgettable hero Storm Westmoreland, in *Riding the Storm*. (A title that should make you go hmmm.) And rounding things out is up-and-coming author Michelle Celmer's second book, *The Seduction Request*.

I would love to hear what you think about Silhouette Desire, so please feel free to drop me a line c/o Silhouette Books, 233 Broadway, Suite 1001, New York, NY 10279. Let me know what miniseries you are enjoying, your favorite authors and things you would like to see in the future.

With thanks,

Melissa Jeglinski

Melissa Jeglinski
Senior Editor
Silhouette Desire

JENNIFER GREENE

Wild
in the
Moment

Silhouette® Desire

Published by Silhouette Books
America's Publisher of Contemporary Romance

SILHOUETTE BOOKS

ISBN 0-373-76622-X

WILD IN THE MOMENT

This edition published by arrangement with Harlequin Books S.A.

® and TM are trademarks of Harlequin Books S.A., used under license.
Trademarks indicated with ® are registered in the United States Patent
and Trademark Office, the Canadian Trade Marks Office and in other
countries.

Visit Silhouette Books at www.eHarlequin.com

Printed in U.S.A.

Books by Jennifer Greene

Silhouette Desire

Body and Soul #263
Foolish Pleasure #293
Madam's Room #326
Dear Reader #350
Minx #366
Lady Be Good #385
Love Potion #421
The Castle Keep #439
Lady of the Island #463
Night of the Hunter #481
Dancing in the Dark #498
Heat Wave #553
Slow Dance #600
Night Light #619
Falconer #671
Just Like Old Times #728
It Had To Be You #756
Quicksand #786
*Bewitched #847
*Bothered #855
*Bewildered #861
A Groom for Red Riding Hood #893
Single Dad #931
Arizona Heat #966
†*The Unwilling Bride* #998
†*Bachelor Mom* #1046
Nobody's Princess #1087
A Baby in His In-Box #1129
Her Holiday Secret #1178
The Honor Bound Groom #1190
***Prince Charming's Child* #1225
***Kiss Your Prince Charming* #1245
§*Rock Solid* #1316
Millionaire M.D. #1340
††*Wild in the Field* #1545
††*Wild in the Mooonlight* #1588
††*Wild in the Moment* #1622

Silhouette Intimate Moments

Secrets #221
Devil's Night #305
Broken Blossom #345
Pink Topaz #418

Silhouette Special Edition

†*The 200% Wife* #1111

Silhouette Books

Birds, Bees and Babies 1990
"Riley's Baby"

Santa's Little Helpers 1995
"Twelfth Night"

Fortune's Children
The Baby Chase

**Jock's Boys*
†*The Stanford Sisters*
§*Body & Soul*
***Happily Ever After*
††*The Scent of Lavender*

JENNIFER GREENE

lives near Lake Michigan with her husband and has two children. She has written more than fifty category romances, for which she has won numerous awards, including three RITA® Awards from the Romance Writers of America in the Best Short Contemporary Books category, and a Career Achievement Award from *Romantic Times* magazine.

One

When Daisy Campbell hit the first patch of black ice, she was tempted to let loose a glass-shattering scream.

She didn't, of course. If she'd learned one thing in the past eleven years, it was to shut up and be careful instead of impulsive—but deep down, she sure *wanted* to scream.

January in Vermont was no new story for her. The wild winds and blizzard snows and bleak-naked trees and mirror-slick roads were as familiar as a tedious TV rerun. It was for reasons like this that she'd left White Hills, Vermont, and never planned to come back.

However, now, in the middle of a life-threatening spin, really didn't seem an ideal time to digress.

The cheap compact she'd rented at the airport was a mighty contrast to the red Ferrari she'd driven on the Riviera, but when push came to shove, a car was a car. The compact spun a complete 360, skidded into the on-

coming traffic lane, and then careened toward the crest
of the hill. Below was an unpleasant drop. Very unpleasant. In fact, unpleasant enough to likely kill her if
she couldn't get the tires to bite—damn soon. Damn,
damn, *damn* soon.

But the tires *did* bite. For a few hairy moments, the
compact faced oncoming traffic, but Daisy battled for
traction and eventually turned the son of a seadog
around. Since no other vehicles were in sight—thanks
to the blizzard—she wasn't hit or harmed. Nothing was
endangered at all, beyond her pulse thumping at sonic-
boom levels, but that was no special event. Her ex-
husband had regularly raised her blood pressure beyond
stroke level easier and faster than any old Vermont blizzard.

It could be that she was getting a tiny bit tired,
though.

The past two months on the Riviera had been a nightmare rather than a vacation. The past two days of solid
traveling and negotiating airports had been nonstop
grueling. And the past two hours, she'd been driving in
escalating ghastly conditions.

The car clock claimed it was three in the afternoon,
but it might as well have been midnight. Black-cheeked
clouds kept rolling in low. The wipers could barely keep
up with the slashing, bashing snow. Drifts were forming
fast, making big, fat white pillows on fence posts and
roofs—but where the wind swept the roads clean, the
surface was slick ice.

Exhausted or not, she simply couldn't relax. Not yet.

Ten minutes from home—even though Daisy hadn't
considered the Campbell homestead to be her real home
for more than a decade—her body seemed to sense the
ordeal was almost over. She couldn't see Firefly Hol-

low, where every teenager in the county traditionally made out on Saturday night, but she knew it was there. She couldn't see Old Man Swisher's pond, either, but growing up, she'd spent so many hours in the neighbor's swimming hole that she knew where it was from the curve in the road. A huge, lioness of a yawn escaped her lungs. Less than a half mile, she'd be home free and safe.

Only, right then, a hundred yards from the driveway, the compact found another diamond slide of ice. It was like trying to control a bullet. She did all the things she was supposed to do, but the little rental car went with the spin, then dove, nose first, into a ditch.

The back tires were still spinning when Daisy let out a long, furious blood-curdling scream.

There were times for impulse control—and times when a woman was justifiably fed-up, ticked-off, had-it, and every other multiple-guess choice there could possibly be.

She turned off the damn car, grabbed her damn purse and overnight bag, and then wrenched open the damn door. Her elegant Italian boots promptly sank into two-foot-deep snow. Naturally she fell. Abandoning all pride, she clawed and crawled her way up from the damn ditch to the damn road.

In that brief period of time, her toes and nose froze solid. Her red cashmere coat and fuzzy hat were designer French; her bags and gloves were Swiss. She'd have traded all of it—including her Manolo Blahnik boots—for a practical L.L. Bean jacket. The kind she grew up in. The kind she swore she'd never wear again as long as she lived.

Eyes squinting against the battering, blustering snow, she trudged toward home. She was exasperated beyond belief, she told herself. Not scared. Daisy Campbell-Rochard-now-Campbell-again simply didn't *do* scared. There was a world of difference between being gutless and being careful. She knew exactly how serious a Vermont blizzard could be. There were snowstorms…and then there were snowstorms—the kind that shut down the community for days. The kind where, if you fell in a drift, no one would likely find you for a good week. The kind where, if you had a brain, you wouldn't be outside at all, much less if you weren't dressed for serious weather.

But then—in spite of the shrieking wind and the fistfuls of snow—she recognized the rail fence. Then the toboggan hill. Then the big old maple tree.

And finally, there it was. Home. The base structure was as old as the first Campbell who came over from Scotland—right after the *Mayflower,* her dad always claimed. Rooms had been added on, but the house was still basically the same sturdy, serious house with white trim and a shake roof. For a moment, fierce, wonderful memories flooded her of coming home other times—smoke puffing from the chimney, lights warming every window, Colin and Margaux flying out the front door to greet their oldest daughter, Violet and Camille laughing and gossiping.

Just that quickly, though, Daisy's heart sank. It didn't *seem* like home when there were no lights, no sign of life. The place looked cold and hauntingly lonely. No one had plowed the road in weeks.

She told herself it was totally stupid to feel at such a loss. Obviously, there couldn't be a welcoming committee when no one knew she was coming home—and she'd known ahead of time that the house was empty.

In fact, when it came down to it, Daisy took a ton of

credit for everyone being so happy and busy these days. Her mom and dad were retired and basking in the Arizona sunshine, thanks to her researching their ideal retirement home.

Camille, the baby of the family, had stopped home for a few months last summer, needing to recover from a god-awful personal tragedy—but Daisy had stepped in there, too, got the family together and organized some subtle matchmaking. Camille and her groom—and his kids and critters and dad—were hanging out in Australia for the next six months.

Violet, their middle sister, had holed up in the farm house for a longer stretch—at least two or three years after getting divorced from the Creep of the Universe. She'd been scaring off men, and likely still would be— if Daisy hadn't stepped in and sent home a man who was brave enough to take her on. Now Vi was married, too, and not as big as a blimp yet, but due in a couple more months. She was living with her new husband somewhere in upstate New York.

Daisy was outstanding at fixing everyone else's lives, if she said so herself. It just never seemed that easy to fix her own—although, to give herself credit, she did learn from her mistakes. If the Adonis of the Universe crossed her path, she wouldn't go out with him for a million dollars.

Five million, even.

But where men were an easy problem to solve—by giving them up, permanently—her current predicament was a little more challenging. Right now she desperately needed to get out of the violent wind and blistering cold before it got any darker, any colder, the snow any deeper. Too fast, scary fast, she was losing feeling in her hands, her feet, her chin. Her fuzzy hat had flown off somewhere, and her hair was wildly whipping around her face.

She battled to get to the back door and then fumbled for the house key in her purse. Her fingers just couldn't seem to function well enough to unsnap the purse, hold the key, aim the key in the lock, turn it.

Finally her fumbling paid off and the door pushed open. Relief surged through her. It was all she needed, all she wanted—home, a place to hole up and hide out for a while. Inside, that awful screaming wind was immediately silenced. The temperature was still freezing, of course, but all she had to do was flick on the furnace, get some hot tea going, get warmed up. Everything was going to be okay.

She dropped her bag and purse, yanked off her snow-crusted gloves, and took her chattering teeth and shaking hands over to the thermostat. She flicked the dial, expecting to hear the gentle woomph of the furnace starting up.

But there was no woomph. No sound at all.

Frowning, she reached for the light switch, thinking that she'd misread the dial in the gloom.

No light turned on. She tried the light over the sink. No light there, either. She flew for the telephone then, but obviously she should have guessed there'd be no functional phone with no one living in the house right now, and she hadn't been home from France long enough to get a cell phone. For a moment she stared blankly around the kitchen, thinking it had been blue and white the last time she'd been home. Now everything was red—red tiles, chintz curtains and rocker cushions. Violet must have done it. The Live Well, Love Much, Laugh Often sign, the girl stuff and country-corny doodads all looked like Violet, too. Daisy didn't care if it wasn't her decorating taste. The drumbeat in her pulse just kept reassuringly thumping *home home home.*

Only she couldn't stay here. If there was no power, no furnace, there was no way to get warm. No way to cook. She couldn't go out in subzero temperatures in the middle of this storm and chop wood. Frantically she jimmied the thermostat dial again, pushing it back and forth, praying for the sound of the furnace. But there was nothing.

Okay, she told herself, *okay,* thinking that if she could just calm down and not panic, she could think up a plan.

No plan emerged. She needed heat. Serious heat. The blizzard could go on for days. She needed heat, food and shelter *now,* before she was any colder, any more exhausted, before the day turned any darker.

For just a second the traitorous thought seeped in her mind that once, just *once* in her life, she'd like a hero. Someone to take care of her for a change. Someone she could depend on. But that thought was so silly that she readily abandoned it.

Daisy had never had a problem attracting men—but they were always the wrong men. The ones she took care of. The ones who were never there when the chips went down. She knew better than to expect anything else, so there was no point in whining—or panicking.

She mentally kicked herself in the fanny and moved. Quickly. All her stuff was being shipped from Europe, but she had the small overnight case. The back hall closet still had some of Dad's old coats, her mom's old boots. There were always spare gloves and hats under the back hall bench. Most of it was older than the hills and worn, but who cared?

She simply had to be covered enough, protected

enough, to get to a neighbor. This was White Hills. No matter what reputation she'd had years ago, there wasn't a soul who wouldn't help a Campbell—or who she wouldn't help, for that matter. The MacDougals were gone, because Camille had married into them. But across the sideroad to the west was the Cunningham Farm. The Cunninghams were old, seventies at least by now. But she knew they'd take her in, and undoubtedly try to feed her. Mr. Cunningham would know something about furnaces. Or he'd have ideas.

She plunked down in the rocker and leaned over to tug off her wonderful—and now ruined—boots. They didn't want to come off. They were frozen to her feet, stiff enough to make tears sting her eyes to get them loose. Beneath, her feet and toes were red as bricks, and stung.

Not good, not good, not good.

Fear was sneaking up, biting at the edges, threatening to overwhelm her if she let it. She wanted to let it. She put on thick old wool socks, her dad's old farm boots, a barn jacket right over her beautiful red cashmere coat. A little warmth started to penetrate, but she wanted to go back in that god-awful screaming wind like she wanted a bullet. It wasn't safe out there, and she knew it.

Still, she swathed her face and neck in a long wool scarf, pulled on double mittens, grabbed her stuff. *Don't think,* she told herself, just *do it.* When she opened the door, the wind and snow slapped her like a bully, trying to scare her again, but she forced herself back down the drive. She'd be okay if she didn't lose her head. It might have been years, but she knew exactly where the Cunningham house was.

God knew how long it took to walk a quarter mile

down the road—an hour? Longer? But finally she saw lights. The lights not only reassured her that the Cunninghams were home, but that they had power, so they must have a generator. A generator meant heat, light, food. Tears of relief stung her eyes as she trudged the last few feet to the back door and thumped with her dad's big mitten.

No one answered.

They were *there*. A pickup was parked in the driveway, buried in snow. Lights lit up the whole downstairs. Come on, come on, Daisy thought desperately. I don't really need a big hero. Just a little one. Just once, just once, just the least little break, and I swear I'll be tough again tomorrow.

She thumped again. Louder. Harder.

Still, no one answered.

Impatiently she turned the knob, and was relieved to find the door unlocked. "Mrs. Cunningham? Mr. Cunningham?" One step inside and she immediately felt the gush of warm, wonderful heat. Nothing and no one could have forced her back out in the cold again. Swiftly she latched the door behind her, still calling out, "Yoo-hoo! It's just me, Daisy Campbell. You know, Margaux and Colin's daughter from across the road. Are you there?"

She heard something. A groan. A man's groan. The sound was so unnerving and unexpected that she responded instinctively by running toward it. Someone sounded hurt. Badly hurt.

She'd been in the Cunninghams' house before, but that was years ago. They had no children of their own, but she'd been there trick-or-treating, selling magazines for school projects, bringing a bushel of apples from her dad's orchard, that kind of thing. She'd never seen the upstairs, but she knew the front hall led to a living room off to the right, then a dining area, then the big, old fashioned kitchen.

The man's groan had seemed to come from the kitchen.

The last time she'd seen it, the room had avocado-green counters and wallpaper with big splashes of orange and green—circa the sixties or seventies—who knew? She'd been a kid, didn't care. Now, though, the kitchen was obviously in the process of a major rehab. A sawhorse and power tools and impressive-looking cords dominated the middle of the room. There was sawdust all over the floor, new counters and cupboards in the process of being installed. Half were done. The ceiling was done, too, except for a light fixture hanging like a drunken sailor. And beneath that, tangled with an overturned ladder, was a man.

Daisy couldn't take in much in that millisecond—just enough to register that he wasn't one of the Cunninghams. The stranger was youngish, somewhere around thirty. She took in his appearance in a mental snapshot—the dark hair, the lean, broad-shouldered build. He was dressed for work, in jeans and a long-sleeved tee, a tool belt slung around his hips. But God. None of that mattered.

He was lying on the dusty, littered floor, his eyes closed, flat on his back. One of his boots was still caught in the rung of a ladder. A pool of blood gleamed beneath his head, shining dark red under the bald lightbulb.

Teague Larson had never gone for angels. It wasn't personal. He'd just always liked sex and sin and trouble too much to waste a lot of time on the saintly types.

On the other hand, he'd never planned on being dead before—and he figured he had to be dead. No one's head could hurt this bad and still be alive. It seemed further proof of his unfortunate demise that the woman had miraculously appeared out of nowhere.

She was so damned gorgeous that he might even forgive her for being an angel. After his head stopped hurting. If his head ever stopped hurting.

It wasn't helping that his personal, breathtakingly unforgettable angel was swearing loudly enough to wake all the rest of the dead.

"Damn it. Damn it. *Damn it.* Does it ever occur to *anybody* that sometime I'd like to be the one who gets rescued? No. Have I ever asked anything from anyone? No. Did I get my sisters married, get my parents retired, get everybody settled? But for Pete's sake, I need a *break* today. The one thing I do *not* need is a problem like you. If you die, I swear, I'm going to kill you, and I'm not kidding! You don't want to see me in a temper. Trust me. You are going to wake up and you're going to be all right, or I swear, you'll be sorry!"

Truth to tell, she wasn't directly talking to him. She just seemed to be shrieking in a top-voice soprano as she flew around the place. He closed his eyes again, willing the room to stop spinning, willing his head to hurt less—at least enough that he could grasp what was going on.

Unfortunately his memory was slowly seeping back in Technicolor and surround sound. Blurry pictures filled his mind of the ladder tipping, then the noisy crash and scrambling fall. It was the worst kind of memory, because it mortifyingly illustrated one guy stubbornly trying to do the job of two. The story of his life. Too much pride. No ability to compromise. Hell, he'd never played well with others in the sandbox.

His personal angel suddenly pushed the ladder out of the way, which jarred his ankle. Until then, he hadn't known his ankle hurt even worse than his head. He'd been better off when he thought he was dead. It'd been quiet around here then. Safer. Now that she'd forced him back to reality, there was no going back to that nice, warm, unconscious place. She'd ruined it.

On the other hand, there seemed to be compensations.

He watched her peel off a silly farmer's hat, shimmy out of an oversize old barn coat, push off clodhopper boots. If he'd had the energy, he'd damn near have gasped at the transformation. He'd already seen she had a gorgeous face, but beneath all that clothing was some kind of guy's favorite secret fantasy.

Deliberately, enticingly, she stroked the front of his pants, clearly trying to get into his pocket. He wasn't in the mood, no, but pain or no pain, a guy could be forced to rise with enough motivation. She was gentle enough, but she was obviously in a rush, hurrying, hurrying, as if she couldn't wait to get her hands on his you-know-what.

Okay, now he knew definitely that he wasn't dead. The view alone inspired him to keep his eyes open, no matter how badly he was hurting. The way her head was bent over him, he saw a tumble of rich, dark hair. Beneath that crazy old farmer's coat was a Christmas-red coat—the kind of thing women looked at in fashion magazines, not the kind of coat people wore in White Hills, Vermont. Didn't matter, she shrugged out of the coat swiftly.

She was stripping for him. Teague told himself his mind was still jangled with pain, but she took off both her coats, hadn't she? And she was still moving, still touching him, still in a big rush. Teague liked to think he'd ignited his share of passion—no lover he'd had ever complained—but he'd never provoked a complete stranger to immediate intimacy before. If he weren't half-dead and more than half-goofy, he'd be loving it. He *was* loving it. He just had a sneaky feeling that he was temporarily a pickle short of a brain. On the other hand, who the hell needed reality?

When she leaned over him, her soft black sweater brushed his cheek. The sweater's V-neck offered him a free look at firm, high breasts. Bountiful breasts. Bountiful, god's-gift-to-a-man, turgid-nippled, plump breasts with the scent of exotic perfume deep in the shadow between them. When she shifted a little, he caught a glimpse of sleek, long legs encased in black pants. A pert little butt.

He liked the legs, but man, that little butt was the sexiest thing he'd seen in months. Maybe years.

He'd only caught a glance at her face before—enough to label her looks striking—but now she turned. Even fantasies weren't this perfect. The skin was smoother than a baby's. A slash of elegant cheekbones had been burned by the wind, the cherry color startling next to all that white skin. A high arch of eyebrows framed big, soft eyes, brown gold like cognac, and her mouth…oh, God, that kissable mouth…

But then he forgot her looks altogether, because her fingers dug really deep into his pocket. Instead of closing her hand around his best friend, though, her fingers emerged into the light, clasping his cell phone.

"Come on," she muttered. "Come on, 911, come on…"

All right, so possibly he wasn't as excited about her

or life as he first thought. His eyelids drooped; he couldn't keep them open. His mind felt as muzzy as steel-wool soup. He heard her voice on the phone, caught partial snatches of her side of a conversation, but he seemed to be uncontrollably fading in and out.

"Sheriff, this is Daisy Campbell...yeah, Margaux and Colin's oldest daughter.... George Webster? You're the sheriff now? Well, that's great, but listen, I..."

She pushed a red-nailed hand through her wild mane of hair. "Yes, I'm back from the south of France. And yes, it's beautiful there. But listen, I..."

She jerked to her feet and spun around, talking faster, appearing more and more agitated. "Yes, I changed my last name back to Campbell. You're right, marriage wasn't for me. Everyone always said that, didn't they? That I'd never settle down..." She seemed to try to interrupt him several more times, and then finally spit out, "*Sheriff!* Would you *listen?* I'm at the Cunningham place. They're not here—"

Again, the person on the other end must have talked some more, because she cut in again. "Well, that's nice to know, that they're vacationing in Pittsburgh, but the *point* is that there's a strange man here.... Teague Larson, you say? Yes. Yes. It does look as if he's a carpenter or electrician or something, but the *point* is that he's *hurt.* Bad hurt. And no, I can't very well calm down and take it easy. I know there's a blizzard but..."

Fade out. Teague tried to catch more, but beneath his eyelids all he could see was a canvas of pea green. Dizzying swirls of pea green. A stomach-churning paisley pattern of swirling pea green.

At some point—who knew how long—he felt her hands on him again. She pulled off his tool belt, which felt a million times better. Smooth, chilled fingers pressed the inside of his wrist, then the carotid artery in his neck. After that, she laid her cheek right on top of his chest, with all that vibrant dark hair tickling his nostrils. Moments passed before she spoke into the cell phone again.

"I can't do a pulse. I'm not a nurse, for Pete's sake. Yes, it seems as if his heart's beating strong, but I have nothing to compare it— *What the Sam Hill do you mean days! I know* we're in the middle of a blizzard. *I don't care.* I want an ambulance here *right now!*"

Okay. If she was going to do the shrieking thing, he was going back to the unconscious thing. Angel or no angel, the pain just wasn't worth it. If she patted him down again, he'd rethink it, maybe wake up again, but until then there just wasn't a lot of motivation to stay with it.

"Damn it, I'm telling you he could be hurt badly! He could have broken bones. And there's blood beneath his head. Okay, okay, I'll…"

More colorful swirls filled his mind. Not pea green this time. More like the blend of colors from stirring whipped cream into coffee. At first the swirling sensation was as fast as a whirlpool, but then everything seemed to slow down, soften, dance to a far quieter tune.

When he heard her voice again, she seemed calmer. At least a little calmer. She'd quit swearing a blue streak at the sheriff, anyway.

"Yeah, I did that. Yeah, okay. I can do that, too. And yes, I can plug in his cell phone somewhere, as long as there's power here. But you have to promise to pick him up as soon as you can. I can keep calling with a report every few hours, but the very *second* you can get an ambulance or Medi-Vac here, I want…"

Teague remembered nothing else for a while. When he woke the next time, shadows had darkened. The wind outside was still howling like a lonely wolf, but the kitchen was completely silent. The naked light fixture over the sink glared straight in his eyes—but not for long.

Huge, gorgeous dark eyes suddenly blocked that sharp, bright light. It was her again. She was real, after all. Who'd ever believe it?

And then there was her voice, not screaming at all now, but low, low as a sexy blues singer, low as sexual promises in the dead of night, whispering an ardent, *"Merde!"*

TWO

Daisy had notoriously bad judgment—and bad luck—with men, but this was ridiculous.

"Even Jean-Luc never put me through this," she muttered. "If I never take care of another man as long as I live, it'll be too soon. I'm not only going to be celibate. I'm going to buy a chastity belt with a lock and no key. I'm going to take antiestrogen pills. Maybe I could try to turn gay. Maybe I could try hypnotism, see if there's a way I could get an automatic flight response near an attractive guy...."

Temporarily she forgot that train of thought, enticing though it was.

Man, she was tired. Her eyes were stinging. Her feet ached. Her heart hurt. She had no battery of energy left, hadn't for the last hour, but it's not as if she had a choice to keep moving.

Crouching down by the fireplace in the Cunningham

living room, she touched a match to kindling, and while waiting to make sure the fire took, mentally ran through a checklist of what still had to be done.

She'd scooped up a box of candles from the Cunninghams' pantry, collected matches, three flashlights, then found a metal tray to put it all in. She located the generator in the basement, which was great, because who knew how long the house would have power? But power, of course, was just the tip of the iceberg.

No one grew up in Vermont without blizzard training. She'd brought in four loads of cut wood from the garage. Stacked it in the living room by the fireplace, then checked the flue and stacked the first branches and kindling. Before starting the fire, though, she'd raided the downstairs closets and cupboards for coats, pillows and blankets. She pulled the curtains and closed all doors to the living room, rolling towels at window and door bases so drafts couldn't get in.

The living room had been updated since the kitchen, judging from the furnishings—which were heavy on the neutrals, and colored up with afghans and pictures and keepsakes. Cluttered or not, Daisy judged it to be potentially the warmest room in the house, which was why she'd set up everything here. It was basic winter storm thinking. Conserve energy. Conserve resources. Not to mention, she didn't want to intrude on the Cunninghams' house or stuff any more than she had to.

All that seemed pretty solid planning—only, she'd been running on fumes for hours now. At least she wasn't still cold, but she was darn close to falling asleep standing up—and there were still three chores she absolutely had to do.

One was fill the bathtubs, for an emergency water

source. The second was food. Soup would do, but she simply had to get something in her stomach soon.

And then there was the other chore.

The kindling took. She watched the little flames lick around the branches, then catch on a small log, and knew her baby fire was going to make it. So she dusted her hands on her fanny and stood up. With a frown deeper than a crater, she aimed for the kitchen.

He was her other chore.

Somehow he had to be moved—but how on earth was she supposed to move a man almost twice as big as she was?

Hands on hips, she edged closer. Long before she'd started the house preparations, she'd tackled what she could for the stranger. Feeling guiltier than a prowler, she'd opened cupboards and drawers until she'd located the Cunninghams' first-aid supplies. As quickly as she could, then, she'd put a clean towel under his head and tried to cleanse the head wound. After that, she tugged off his boots. He'd groaned so roughly when she touched his right foot that she'd gingerly explored, pulling off his sock—and found one ankle swollen like a puff ball.

Great. Another injury. She'd wrapped the ankle with some tape—God knew that might be the wrong thing if he had a broken bone. But doing nothing seemed the worse choice, so she kept moving, packed the ankle in some ice, then covered him with a light blanket for shock. For quite a while she just stayed there with him, hunkered down, worried sick he was going to die on her—until she realized she was acting like a scared goose.

She wasn't helping him, staying there and tucking the blanket around him another dozen times. The only thing she *could* do was get her butt in gear and do some survival preparation stuff. So she'd done all that, but now...

Damn. She couldn't just leave him on the hard kitchen floor. It was drafty, cold, dirty. The couch or carpet in the living room was warmer, safer, more protected.

But how to move him, without moving his right ankle or his head? How to move his weight at all?

She thought, then trekked upstairs, thinking Mrs. Cunningham had to have a linen closet somewhere. She found it and pulled a sheet from the bottom shelf, hoping it wasn't a good one. The plan was to somehow wrestle him onto the sheet, with the hope that she'd be able to pull him across the floor that way.

If that didn't work... But she amended that thought. It *had* to work. She had no other ideas.

Crouching down, she gently pushed and prodded until she'd maneuvered the sheet under his weight. It took a while, partly because she was so worried about injuring him further, and partly because she kept glancing at his face.

He took her breath away; she had to admit it. He just had the kind of looks that really rang her chimes. Rugged jaw, dusted with whiskers. The kind of thick, rough hair that never stayed brushed, not too short, not too styled, just...himself. Shoulders that wouldn't be subdued in an ordinary shirt. Jeans worn soft, the kind that said he didn't give a damn what they looked like.

Physical, she thought dispassionately. One look, and she could immediately picture him hot and sweaty, throwing a woman on the bed and diving in after her. The kind of guy who was lusty about sex, lusty about life, lusty about everything he did. Bullheaded. Those kinds of guys always were. The thicker the neck, the more stubborn the brain. And the bigger the feet, the bigger... Well, it wasn't as if she cared how big he was under that zipper.

She was immune. She could look, she could enjoy— as long as he stayed alive for her, anyway. But she already knew he was totally wrong for her. She didn't know why at that precise moment. Maybe he was married. Or maybe he couldn't define *faithful* with a big-print dictionary. Or maybe he'd found some creative, new way to break a woman's heart.

The details didn't matter.

The reality was that she had never—ever—fallen for a good guy. The flaw was in her, not them. She had some kind of chemistry surge near bad boys. The difference between when she was seventeen and now, though, was that she faced her problems. No more ducking or denial.

Which meant that when and if she liked the looks of a guy, that was it—she shut the barn door and padlocked it.

Right now, though, she couldn't be worried less about falling for Mr. Adorable. She was focused on one goal and one goal only—which was to pull the big guy into the living room before she collapsed from 1) a broken back, 2) exhaustion, 3) starvation, or 4) all of the above. My God, he was heavy. Sweat prickled the back of her neck. She pulled with all her might, groaning to give herself extra strength, and still only managed to drag him a few more inches.

Jean-Luc, her ex, had less character than a boa constrictor. But at least he'd been relatively light. Even when he'd been three sheets to the wind—or high—

he'd usually been able to at least *help* her move him around. This guy...

When she glanced down at him again, the guy in question not only seemed to be conscious, but was staring with fascination at her face. "Not that I mind being carried...but wouldn't it be easier for me to get up and walk?" he asked.

She couldn't kill him. No matter how mad she was, you just couldn't murder a man who was already hurt. But an hour later she was still ticked off.

That was also the soonest she could find time to close the door on the kitchen and call the sheriff to make another report.

"I hear you, George," she said into the receiver. "And I admit it. He's alive. I even admit that it doesn't look as if he's going back into a coma anytime soon. But I still have no way to know how badly hurt he is. I need an ambulance. Or a helicopter. Or a snowmobile—"

While she listened, she also ground a little fresh pepper onto the potato soup. The stove and refrigerator were still functioning in the torn-up kitchen, but that was about it. There was no sink or running water. All the pots and pans and dishes had been moved elsewhere, ditto for silverware, food and spices.

Daisy considered herself outstanding at making something out of nothing—not because she'd ever wanted that talent, but God knows, because being married to Jean-Luc had required some inventive scrambling to just survive. She'd always been her mom's daughter in the kitchen, besides. So she started out with a bald can of potato soup she found in a basement pantry, then found kitchen tools and the spices in boxes in the dining room, then raided the depths of the fridge, finally came through with some bacon crumbs and a beautiful hunk of cheddar.

The chives and pepper weren't as fresh as she'd like, but a decent soup was still coming together. If she could just get rid of her unwanted invalid, she might even be able to relax.

"Yes, George, I hear that wind outside. And I can't even see for the snow. But that's why you guys have snow machines, isn't it? To be able to rescue people in all conditions? No, I'm not exaggerating! At the very least, he needs some X-rays. And some antibiotics or medicine like that—oh, for Pete's sake." She stared in disbelief at the cell phone. "*No,* I won't go out with you when this is all over, you…you cretinous *canard! Des clous!*"

The French insults didn't even dent his attitude. George just laughed. The sheriff! The one person in town who was supposed to rescue you no matter what the problem!

When it came down to it, the law had never done her a lick of good.

The soup was finally ready. She wrapped a spoon in a napkin, flicked off the kitchen light and carried her steaming bowl into the living room. The fire was popping-hot now. She'd have to wake up in the night to make sure it was fed—otherwise it'd go out, and suck all their warmth out the chimney. But for now, the cherry and apple logs smelled as soothing as an old-fashioned Christmas.

She ignored the shrieking wind, as easily as she ignored the long, blanket-covered lump on the couch. Darn it, she'd earned this meal. And she was actually getting woozy-headed from exhaustion and jet lag and too many hours without something in her stomach.

Quickly she settled in the giant recliner—obviously Mr. Cunningham's favorite chair, judging from the hunting magazines stacked next to it—and reached for the spoon.

A sexy voice—a pitiful, weak, vulnerable but nevertheless sexy voice—piped up from the deep shadows of the couch. "Could I have just a little of that?"

"No."

A moment passed, and then the voice piped up again, this time adding a desperate, ingratiating tone on top of the weak and pitiful. "It smells really good. In fact, it smells fantastic."

"Tough. You're not getting any food."

When he responded with silence again this time, she had to relent. "Look. I'm not eating in front of you to be mean. There's nowhere to sit in the kitchen and I'm beat and this is the only other room that's really warm. Honestly, though, it's just not a good idea for you to have food after a head bump. You could throw up."

Like any other guy who'd made it to first base, he immediately tried for second. "I won't. I promise I won't."

"So you say. But the sheriff said I was to make sure you stayed awake, check your pupils every couple of hours and not give you any food until tomorrow morning." She scooped up more soup, still not looking at him. She still remembered the ka-boom of her heartbeat when she half carried the big lug into the living room. Then she'd had to suffer through a whole bunch more intimate body contact in the process of settling him on the couch and tucked him in again.

That was her whole problem with men. They looked at her a certain way, she caved. He was one of them, she could sense it, smell it, taste it. For right now at least he was hurt. How much damage could a guy do when he was hurt? Particularly when she refused to look at him. She wasn't volunteering for any more of those ka-booms.

"Please," he begged charmingly.

She plunked down her soup, growled a four letter word in total disgust, then marched into the kitchen to spoon out another bowl. A *small* bowl. She brought it back with a scowl. "You get two spoonfuls. No more."

"Okay."

"You keep that down, then we'll talk. But I don't want to hear any whining or bribes."

"No whining. No bribes. Got it," he promised her.

Yeah. That big baritone promising not to whine was like a bear promising not to roar, but she slid the ottoman over and sat down with the bowl. "Don't try sitting. Just lean up a little bit."

"I think there's a slim chance I could feed myself."

"I think there's a big chance you'll eat the whole bowl. That's the point. I'm controlling this."

"Ah. A bossy, controlling woman, are you?"

"No. A scared woman. If you die or get hurt any worse, I'm going to be stuck with you until this blizzard is over." She lifted the spoonful, and he obediently opened his mouth, his eyes on hers. Again she told herself he was *hurt,* for Pete's sake. But how the hell could an injured guy have so much devilment in those eyes?

"Are we going to sleep together in here?"

She sighed, then plugged his mouth with another spoonful. "When *I'm* hurt," she said pointedly, "I usually make an extra point of being nice to the people who are stuck taking care of me."

"Well, if you won't sleep with me, would you consider taking a shower with me? Because I've got sawdust itches from my neck to my toes. My hands are full of grit. I just want to clean up.''

"No showers. No baths. What if you fell?'' But when she fed him another spoonful, she had to consider the thought. "It *could* be a good idea to make sure there isn't any dust or debris near that head wound, though.''

"Yeah, that's what I was thinking. And I couldn't fall if you took the shower with me. Maybe if we got around to formally introducing ourselves? I'm Teague Larson—''

"I know. The sheriff told me. And I'm Daisy Campbell. You can either call me Daisy—or Battle-Ax—but either way, no shower. I'll try to cook up some way to get your hands clean. If we still have water and power tomorrow, maybe we can talk about a shower for you then. But tonight we're doing what the sheriff said for a concussion.''

"I don't have a concussion.''

"You knocked yourself out. You could very well have a concussion,'' she corrected him.

"I knocked myself out because I was an idiot, took a chance I shouldn't have taken. But my head's too hard to dent, trust me, or ask anyone who knows me. In the meantime, I don't suppose there's any more soup? Or any real food somewhere?''

"The kitchen's a complete disaster—which you should know, since you're the one who tore it up. I was lucky to find the soup and a pot to put it in. You're not getting any meat or heavy foods, anyway, so don't waste your breath looking at me like that.''

"Like what?''

She fed him one more spoonful of soup, then ignored those soulful eyes and carted the dishes into the downstairs bathroom. Without running water in the kitchen,

she was stuck doing dishes in the bitsy bathroom sink—
but that was the end of the chores. She could still do a
dozen more things to prepare for a loss of power, but
they just weren't going to happen. She was two seconds
away from caving.

When she returned to the living room, she brought
the invalid a fresh glass of water and a warm washcloth
to wipe his hands, then knelt at the hearth. Once the
fire was tended, she fully intended to sink into a night-
long coma. The blaze was going strong, but she needed
to poke the fattest logs, tidying up the bed of ashes, add
on two more slow-burning logs.

"The way you talked to the sheriff, you seemed to
know him." Teague, darn him, sounded wide awake.

"George Webster? I went to school with him." She
hung up the poker and turned around. "He followed me
around my whole senior year with his tongue hanging
out."

There, she'd won a grin. His eyes tracked her as she
pushed off her shoes and shook out a blanket. "I'll bet
a lot of boys followed you with their tongues hanging
out," he said wryly.

"A few," she admitted. "What kills me now is re-
alizing how immature I was. I wanted the guys to like
me. I wanted a reputation for being wild and fun. And
whether that was dumb or not, I had two younger sisters, both of whom looked up to me. I should have been
thinking about being a role model for them, and instead…"

"Instead what?"

"Instead…" She curled up in the overstuffed recliner
and wrapped the blanket around her. God knew why
she was talking. Probably because she was too darn
tired to think straight. "Instead there was only one thing

in my head in high school. Getting out. I couldn't wait to grow up and leave White Hills and do something exciting. I was never in real trouble—not like trouble with the police. But someone was always calling my mom on me. My skirt was too short. My makeup was too 'artsy.' I'd skip English to hang out in the Art Room. I never did anything *big* wrong, but I can see now it was all just symbolic little stuff to show how trapped I felt in a small town and how much I wanted to leave.''

''Yet now you're back.''

''Only for a short time. I just need a few weeks to catch my breath before moving on again.'' Even though her eyes were drooping, she could hear the ardent tone in her voice. She so definitely wasn't staying. A few hours back in White Hills, and already she'd been caught up in a blizzard and a guy problem. It was a sign. She should never have tried coming home. Even for a month. Even knowing she'd been pretty darn desperate.

''If you don't mind my asking, how did you come to be living in the south of France?''

Her eyes popped open—at least temporarily. Maybe tiredness had loosened her tongue, but she couldn't fathom how he'd known she lived in France.

He explained, ''Pretty hard not to know a little about you. You're one of the exotic citizens of White Hills, after all. Daisy Campbell, the exotic, glamorous, adventurous girl...the one all the other girls wanted to be, who had the guts to leave the country and go play all over France with the rich crowd....''

''Oh, yeah, that's sure me,'' she said wryly, and washed a hand over her face. Sometimes it was funny, how you could say a fact, and it really was a fact—yet

it didn't have a lick of truth to it. She hadn't been playing in a long time. Anywhere. With anyone. "Anyway…I ended up living in France because I fell in love
with an artist. Met him at one of his first American
shows, which happened to be in Boston. I can't even
remember why I was visiting there…but I remember
falling in love in about two seconds flat. Took off and
married him right after high school."

"I take it he was French?"

"Yeah, he was French. And he wanted to live in Aix-
en-Provence, where Cézanne had studied with Emile
Zola. And then Remy-en-Provence, where Van Gogh
hung out for a long time. And then the Côte d'Azur—
because the light on the water is so pure there, or that's
what all the artists say, that there's no place like the
French Riviera."

"Hmm…so you traveled around a lot. Sounds ritzy
and exciting."

"It was," she said, because that's what she always
told everyone back home. They thought she was glori-
ously happy. They thought she was living a glamorous,
always-exciting dream of a life. No one knew otherwise—except probably her mother, and that was only
because Margaux had the embarrassing gift of being
able to read her daughters' minds.

"So…are you still married to this artist?"

"Nope. Pretty complicated getting a divorce for two
people of different citizenships, but that's finally done
now. And I don't know exactly what I'm doing after
this, but you can take it to the bank, I'm never living
anywhere but my own country again." She opened her
eyes. Somehow, even now, she seemed to feel obligated
to say something decent about her ex-husband. "My ex
really was and *is* a fine artist. That part was totally the

real thing. He wasn't one of those artists who have to die to make it. His work's extraordinary, been recognized all over the world. Jean-Luc Rochard. You might have seen his paintings."

"Not me. The only original artwork I've got are those paint-by-number-kit things. Oh. And a black-velvet rendition of Elvis."

Darn it. He'd made her chuckle again. "Got a houseful of those, do you?"

"Maybe not a houseful." She felt his gaze on her face in the firelight. "So…what happened?"

"What happened when?"

"What happened, that you got a divorce. You talk up the guy like he was the cat's meow, a woman's romantic dream. And you were living the high life in fantastic places. Yet something obviously had to go wrong, or you'd still be with him."

"Oh, no. I've spilled all I'm going to spill for one night. Your turn next. And if this storm is going to be anywhere near as bad as I'm afraid of, we'll be marooned here for another day or two—so we'll have more time to talk than either of us probably wants. For the immediate future—do you need a trip to the library but are too embarrassed to tell me?"

"I'll deal with a trek to the library after you go to sleep."

"Well, that's the problem, Mr. Teague Larson," she said patiently. "I'm completely dead on my feet. Which means I'm going to conk out in this chair any second now. I'm supposed to call the sheriff every few hours, report how you are. And I'm supposed to wake you up every two hours and look in your eyes, check the size of your pupils. Only, I'm afraid that I'm not going to get either of those things done. I'm losing it, I can tell.

So if you need some help getting into the bathroom, you need to tell me now.''

''I don't need help.''

''Yeah, you do. But I'm not up for bullying you. I'm warning you, this is your last call for free help.'' She yawned, as if to punctuate how tired she was. And that was the last thing she remembered.

Three

Teague had to grin. When that woman slept, she slept. She'd been right in the middle of talking when her eyelids suddenly closed and she snugged her cheek in the side of the chair. Two blinks later she was snoring. Not big, noisy, guy snores, but whispery little snores. The kind a woman makes when she was end-of-her-rope tired.

Teague figured it was the perfect time to hightail it into the bathroom—finally. Contrary to what Daisy thought, he wasn't embarrassed. He was a grown man, for heaven's sake. But the truth was, the only way he could make it into the bathroom was by crawling on all fours. The bump on his head ached and stung, but that wasn't the worst problem. As long as he only moved slowly—and didn't laugh—the head wound wasn't bugging him too much. His swollen right ankle was giving him fits, though. At least for tonight there was no chance of his walking on it.

Teague had asked for help in his life. He was almost sure of it, even if he couldn't remember a single occasion specifically. For damn sure, though, he wasn't asking a woman, as if he were some kind of needy, sickly, dependent type.

So he crawled into the bathroom, at an extremely annoying snail's pace. Then he had to sit on the blue-tiled floor until his head stopped spinning and he stopped sweating from the exertion. Eventually, though, he took care of nature, brushed his teeth, managed a reasonably efficient sponge bath, and then crawled back into the living room.

The wind howled louder than ever, or maybe the intense darkness made it seem that way. Eerie shrieky sounds seemed to seep through the walls and whistle through the cracks. Teague hesitated at the couch, but rather than climb back up there, he carted the pillow and blanket closer to the fire. The yellow blaze was dancing-hot, but wouldn't last all night. He figured he could feed it easier through the wee hours if he was already located on the carpet, closer to the hearth.

He used a log from the stack of cut wood to elevate his right leg, and then sank back against the blanket. Just when he thought the setup was perfect and he could doze off, he realized that he couldn't see Daisy's face from that angle—her whole body was in shadow. That wouldn't do, so he had to refix the log and blankets and pillow all over again.

By then he was wasted-tired and getting cranky from the day's various aches and injuries. But he could see her. If a guy had to be miserable, she was the best diversion he could conceivably imagine.

There were dark shadows under those gorgeous eyes. Didn't matter. She'd be striking if she were dead-sick with the flu. She had the bones, the style, the attitude. No one was going to miss noticing Daisy Campbell— at least no guy was, not in this life.

She wasn't, though, even remotely the way she billed herself.

For a woman who complained about being stuck with him—and yelled loudly to the sheriff how desperate she was to get him off her hands—she didn't act remotely thrown about taking responsibility for an injured stranger. In fact, she was taking no-fanfare, no-fuss, damn good care of him. She also acted sassy and snappy, but those hands of hers were gentle and so was the concern in her eyes.

Every contradiction seemed more interesting than the last. For a woman who looked as if French couture was her *raison d'être,* she sure made a feast out of an ordinary cup of potato soup. And although she carried herself as if a ton of servants usually trailed after her, she'd shown a ton of practical common sense about storm survival.

He didn't get it.

He didn't get her.

Something strange was happening here. Really strange. Teague didn't like surprises. He didn't mind being attracted to her—hell, no man had control over that. His you-know-what couldn't tell whether a woman was potentially catastrophic or not. But his brain did.

She'd given him the message loud and clear that she was a rolling stone.

He'd fallen in love with one of those once before. Had no reason to volunteer to be kicked in the head a second time.

Still. There was no harm in just looking at that spec-
tacularly interesting face. It was one of those favorite
guy fantasies, being marooned with a beautiful woman
with no one else around. It's not as if there were any
chance of their getting close. Hell, he couldn't imagine
laying a finger on her.

Teague couldn't have closed his eyes, because that
howling wind was itching on his nerves, and he hurt in
too many places to really rest.

But suddenly his eyes opened. Any man's would. Because out of nowhere there seemed to be an extremely
warm, mobile, voluptuous woman plastered against
him.

More than his eyes popped up, in fact. It occurred to
him that the same woman pressing warm, firm, full
breasts against his chest and winding a leg around his
hip, was precisely the same one he'd just sworn—seconds before—that he'd never lay a finger on.

"You're awake, Teague? Don't get shook. It's just
me."

Maybe it was pitch-black in the room, give or take
the yellow firelight behind the screen, but he fully, fully
realized who was wrapped around him.

"We lost power. Since it was already down across
the road, it's really amazing we had it this long—especially in this kind of snowstorm. When it's morning
and there's more light, I'll go down to the basement,
see if I can get the Cunninghams' generator fired up.
For right now, though, we're sealed up in this room as
tightly as we can be. I know it's cold and getting colder.
The fire alone can't keep up with subzero temperatures
like this. But if we stay close, combine blankets and
body heat, we'll be fine."

"Okay."

"We could be snowed in for a couple more days, but there's no way it'll be longer than that before someone comes to rescue you. We've got food and water and firewood. We may be cold, but we'll be able to manage."

"Okay."

"Nothing's going to happen to you. I know you're hurt. Being stranded has to feel a lot more unnerving if you're hurt. But I lived in Vermont my whole life. I can do whatever we both need doing. Don't worry."

"I wasn't worried."

"I realize this has to be uncomfortable for you—"

In spite of his pounding head and throbbing ankle, he reached over and kissed her. He wasn't trying to shut her up. He didn't give a damn if she talked and kept them both up all night. But he did mind her treating him as if he were a schoolboy who needed nonstop reassurance.

The kiss might have been impulsive, but it still seemed a reasonable, logical way to tactfully let her know he was a man, not a boy.

And that seemed the last reasonable, logical, tactful thought he had for a long time. Seconds. Minutes. Maybe even hours.

She was cold. Heaven knew how long she'd been freezing up in that chair, but her lips were chilled, her hands even more so. The instant his mouth connected with hers, though, she stopped moving altogether. She seemed to even stop breathing. Her eyes popped wide. His were already open, waiting for her. Both of them were suddenly frowning at each other in the shadow of the blankets.

There was a lot to frown about, Teague acknowledged, since they were obviously near-complete strangers, and neither expected any problem with intimacy. At least he hadn't, for damn sure—but now he'd tasted her, he had to go back for another kiss.

She tasted like sleepy woman. Thick. Sweet. Her neck had the barest hint of scent. Not perfume exactly, but the echo of something clean and natural and soft…lavender, he thought. A whisk of spring in a night that couldn't have been darker or colder.

And that was the last time either of them had to worry about the cold night. Body heat suddenly exploded between them. They could hardly move under their combined blankets, which was almost funny, since neither suddenly needed any of that blanket heat, anyway.

This wasn't him, wildly kissing her, recklessly running his hands down her lithe, supple body. It couldn't be. He wasn't remotely a wild or impulsive man. He was the kind of man who paid attention to every detail, who did things right and thoroughly. But damn. Right then there were only two of them in a winter wilderness. A caveman who'd drawn his chosen mate under his bed of furs.

If she accidentally kicked his ankle, he'd undoubtedly cry like a baby.

But until then, the caveman thing was taking over his head, his hormones, his pulse. Either that or the taste of her, the touch of her, was acting like an uncontrollable fever. He didn't respond to a woman like this. A few kisses never packed this kind of punch. And sex—the kind of sex that mattered, that pulled out all the stops—only happened between two people who knew each other damn well.

He didn't know her at all.

But it felt as if he did. Maybe his reaction was explainable, two people caught in extraordinary circumstances, but it felt…she felt…as if no other woman had ever touched him. She made an oomph sound, a groan, when his mouth chased after hers yet another time. Lips teased, trembled together, then parted. Her tongue was already waiting for his.

Her rich, thick hair shivered through his fingers as he cradled her head, holding her securely to take her mouth, to dive for that sweetness again. She was already surfing on that channel. Her arms wound around him, tugged around him, as if she could anchor him to her. Through tons of blankets, tons of clothes, he could still feel her breasts throbbing, heating against his chest. Still feel the tension in her long, slim legs, still feel the chaotic burn, the urgency, of a connection neither wanted to break.

There'd been no one who kissed like her, and Teague sensed, never would be, never could be. Maybe he'd survive without another taste, but he couldn't swear to it.

The fire sizzled and spit.

Dark shadows danced on the walls.

Blankets tangled and fought. His head, his ankle…both hurt. But not like the ache building deep in his groin. This was champagne he'd never tasted, a high he'd never expected. It pulled at him.

She pulled at him.

He didn't believe for a second that she intended to respond this way. Wildly. No inhibitions. Just need, hanging as naked between them as secrets. Longings bursting to the surface because no one thought they'd needed a lock to protect them, not this night, not this way.

She'd been through hell. She'd never said that exactly—but it was there, in her eyes, her touch, that kind of urgent take-me-take-me-because-I-want-the-hurt-to-go-away. He knew the words to that song. When you were hurt, you wrapped yourself up tight, so the wounds had a chance to heal. You'd have to be crazy to ask for a fresh hurt before the old scars healed up…yet loneliness was always the worst when you'd been hurt. It took you down. Made you doubt whether anyone'd ever be there for you again. Made you worry what was wrong with you, that someone you'd given your best to hadn't loved you enough.

Hell. He not only knew that song. He knew the refrain and every verse. But as he increasingly sensed her vulnerability…he was stuck increasingly sensing his own.

He tore his mouth free from her, tried to gulp in some oxygen, when all he really wanted to do was gulp in her. Now. All night. Forever, and then all over again. "Daisy…"

"I know. This is insane." She was struggling for oxygen just as he was, looking at him with dazed dark eyes. "But damn. I just wasn't expecting this."

"Neither was I."

"Do you always kiss this well, or am I just really fantastic at bringing it out in you?"

"Um, something tells me there's no way I can answer that question without getting my head smacked."

Gentle fingers lifted to his cheek. "I wouldn't hit you in the head, *cher*. Not when you're already wounded. I wouldn't do anything worse than slug you in the stomach, and that's a promise."

"Thanks. I think."

"We're both getting some common sense back, aren't we."

"Yeah," he said regretfully.

"I'm up for doing impulsive things. For going with the moment. For living. But maybe…this is just a little too impulsive."

"I know." But he still couldn't keep the regret out of his voice. "I never do stupid things."

"No? Well, heaven knows, I do. I've made so many stupid, impulsive mistakes that really, I could give courses in blundering the wrong way through life. I could teach you how."

"From you," he said, "I'd like to learn."

She chuckled, a seductive whisper from her throat. "How about if I promise, Teague, that sometime during this blizzard…"

He waited to hear the end of her comment. And when she said nothing else he tilted his head so he could easily see her face.

The eyes were shut, little breathy snores sneaking from her damp, parted lips again. She'd fallen asleep. Just like that. Leaving him harder than stone and with an unnamed promise.

He hoped to hell that wasn't an omen.

Daisy vaguely heard the cell phone ringing. Jet lag and exhaustion had taken her down so deep she couldn't seem to jolt herself awake. It was cold. Her brain got that right away. It was also daylight, because the unfamiliar room was much lighter than the night before.

Slowly more reality managed to bully itself into her mind, forcing her to seriously wake up. She was at the Cunninghams'. She'd kissed the stranger. She was in the middle of a blizzard. Damn, had she *ever* kissed the stranger. The fire was still going strong, ashes piled deep and glowing, fresh fed fairly recently—by someone who wasn't her. She'd not only kissed the stranger lying next to her, she'd come on to him like a fresh-freed nun. Her family was all out of town; she was broke as a church mouse; her entire life was in shambles. She seemed to be *still* wrapped around Teague Larson as if they were glued at the hip and pelvis.

And it was his cell phone ringing, demanding someone get up.

She pushed out of the blankets, had the cold air slap at her skin and decided that a girl only needed so much reality.

"Yeah," she snapped at the sheriff when she finally grabbed Teague's cell phone in the kitchen. "I'm well aware the power's off, George. I'm going to look this morning to see if I can get the Cunninghams' generator going. If I can't, then I'll bring in the wood from their garage. No, I don't know how my patient's doing…."

Blah, blah, blah. Twenty-three inches of snow. Still snowing, not as hard, but big winds, some six- and seven-foot drifts. The town was busted except for absolute emergencies for a few days. Like everyone in Vermont couldn't guess the day's news report?

She yawned, then waited until she could get a word in. "All right, all right. So we're not on a level of heart attacks and babies being born. But Teague really was hit hard on the head. And I know his ankle's hurt. You keep us on the rescue list, you hear? And, yeah, I'll check in a little later today, so you know how we're doing."

As she walked back in the living room, she reminded herself to contact her parents and sisters pretty quickly. They didn't know she was back home in White Hills. She also hadn't told them the whole story of her divorce from Jean-Luc, but that was a different issue. The only immediate problem was if they tried to reach her in France and couldn't, they'd worry.

She raked a hand through her sleep-tumbled hair, her mind still galloping a zillion miles an hour, then stopped dead.

So did Teague.

For some unknown reason he was on his hands and knees, emerging from the back of the couch like a little kid playing hide-and-seek—at least until she spotted him. Or he spotted her. Whichever came first, both of them seemed to freeze in unison.

Daisy didn't move, but her pulse suddenly lunged—just as it had last night when she'd touched him. When she'd judiciously crawled under the blankets with him to conserve heat. When she'd extremely unjudiciously started running her hands all over the man. It was as if someone had taken over her mind. How else could she explain how this confounding man had her hormones in such a buzz?

"What are we doing?" she asked tactfully, since he didn't seem to be moving from his crawling position.

"I was looking for something behind the couch."

"Uh-huh."

"I dropped something out of my pocket last night. A key. It's not like I needed it this minute, but when I realized it was missing, I thought I'd better find it before I forgot—"

She cut to the chase. "Your ankle is that bad? You can't walk on it at all?"

He scowled at her. He had no way of knowing that she'd been lied to by the best. Her ex could lie to the Pope on Easter and look innocent.

"I can walk on it," Teague said irritably.

"I'll tell you what," she said. "You crawl to the

bathroom—in fact, we'll call that *your* bathroom for the duration. I'll use the one upstairs. No more showers or cleaning up for either of us, though, until the power goes back on, okay? But the point is—''

"There's a point coming?"

"The point is, I'll try and rig you up some kind of cane. And some ibuprofen. When you get back, you go for the couch, we'll get your weight off the ankle and ice it."

"I can do all that."

He kept singing that refrain all day. Daisy might have become exasperated except that, damn, he kept getting cuter by the hour. Every time she started to do something, he crawled after her, determined to either help or do it himself. After being prey to the most dependent guy in the universe for the past several years, Teague's bullheadedness was a treat.

"I *know* how to get the generator started," he said.

"I'm sure you do. And it's been years since I watched my dad do ours when we were growing up. I'm not sure I remember what he did, or that I can do it besides. But the generator's still in the basement."

"So?"

"So you can't get down to the basement with that ankle. So it has to be me. *Go sit on that couch.*"

"I'll sit at the top of the stairs in case you come up with questions."

She screwed off the sweeper end of a broom to create a makeshift cane. Brought in another load of logs. Tended the fire. Battled the generator in the basement, couldn't figure it out, braved Mr. Cunningham's desk to see if she could find a file of appliance instructions, tried a second time to get the generator going. Failed again.

So they were going to be cold. At least they had the
fire and firewood. Nobody was going to get frostbite or
die or anything. But if the darn wind would quit howling and the sky quit dumping buckets, the power would
have a chance to come back on. Then the snowstorm
would just be a pain in the behind, but not really uncomfortable.

"I can go down in the basement," Teague argued
again.

"Yes. But what if you fell on that ankle? I couldn't
possibly carry you back upstairs."

"I wouldn't fall."

He was so male. Only a male would make such a
ridiculous statement. By that time she'd fixed them both
an early dinner. "Eat," she said, looking to divert him.

It worked. She looked at the wound on his head every
time she could sneak a glance—which wasn't easy,
when he kept claiming it was fine. It wasn't remotely
fine. The gash was a good three inches, with a lump
under it that looked bruised and swollen. On the other
hand, she reasoned, he couldn't be too injured if he
could eat like a wolf at his last meal.

"I don't understand how you could make this out of
a nonexistent kitchen," he said.

"Are you kidding? This is the kind of cooking that's
all fun. You get to use your imagination instead of just
opening a can and punching a microwave." Truthfully,
he was giving her a bunch of unwarranted praise. She
hadn't been that creative, just unearthed some clothes
hangers to twist into spits, then raided the Cunninghams' freezer for a couple of steaks. She was going to
owe them all kinds of supplies when this was over with.
Anyway, she'd rubbed some garlic and tarragon and a
few other surprises on the steaks. Wrapped some pota-

toes in foil. Added this and that. The thing was, everything always tasted good by fire. It's not as if she'd pulled off a miracle.

"It wouldn't be so hard if we just got the generator going. I *know* I could do it—''

That again. If she kept him out of the basement, it'd be a miracle. She tried diverting him again. "So exactly how did you get into the demolition business?''

"Demolition?''

"Yeah. You know. Tearing up kitchens. Tearing down walls. Getting to use power tools all day, make noise and lots of sawdust. I mean, have you always had this calling, or did you just never grow up?''

He almost choked—but Teague, it was clear, was never going to waste a good bite of steak, even when he had to fight not to laugh.

"I was playing with wood from the time I was a little kid. Couldn't shake the love for it, so made a career out of it. The Cunningham job, though, was more a favor than the kind of work I normally do. They were going to be out of town for a few weeks, so I could fill in here when I had time from other projects. Mostly, though, I do reconstruction stuff. Old wood. Uneven floors. Tilted ceilings. Ruined woodwork—''

She could hear the joy building up in his voice like an opera singer letting loose with an aria. "Now, don't go have an orgasm on me.''

He grinned. "I can't help it. That's the stuff that pulls my chain. I went to college to be a lawyer. Just wasn't for me, hated every minute of it. Went back to do the apprentice thing with a master carpenter.''

"So. Why are you working solo and how on earth did you get stuck in White Hills?''

"What makes you think I'm stuck?''

"Because I know you didn't start out here. I'd have known you—we'd have gone to school together. Or I think we would have. How old are you?"

"Thirty-four."

"A few years older than me. Which means I'd definitely have known you, because I knew every cute boy who was a few years older than me. And I'll bet you were downright adorable in high school, because you're so delectable now."

That almost made him choke on his food a second time. "Campbell, you are one bad, bad woman. You always tease like this?"

"Good grief, no. Only with people I'm stranded with. Especially when I'm stranded with someone for an unknown period of time without deodorant or enough water to take a shower."

"There's deodorant in the downstairs bathroom."

She lifted a brow. "There's some upstairs, too. I was just trying to make the subtle point that we're stuck with each other for company, so we might as well enjoy it. Which means I think you should tell me why in God's name you picked a rustic village like White Hills to live."

"Hey, there are lots of old homes here. Homes, historic buildings, stores, churches. And that's what I love best. Restoring stuff. Not necessarily restoring it back to how it looked historically, but taking something that's turned ugly and bringing it back to life."

"That's cool. But you couldn't find any place more exciting than White Hills?"

"Maybe I didn't want to."

"Maybe you're hiding a deep, dark secret," she suggested instead.

He looked amused at her nosiness. "For the record, I'm making money hand over fist in your little burg."

"That's nice. But it doesn't answer the question why you picked this town to live in."

"I had a job here once, liked the place. And since moving here about five years ago, I've built up more work than I know what to do with. The only thing really holding me back is being so unartsy."

She cocked her head. "You need to be artsy to be a carpenter?"

"Not always. I mean, give me a kitchen, a blank room, and I'll come up with a floor plan, a way to use the existing features and space to make the most of it. I love that kind of creative work. But these days, people hire someone for a major restoration project, they really like all the experts in one basket. I'm first fiddle in the carpentry department. But when they want me to pick a color for a wall, or what knobs on a door, or what furniture to go with the floor…hell, I don't see why they want decorator stuff from me. But that's the part I'm missing. Assuming I wanted my business to grow. Which I don't. But sometimes that does hold me back."

"So hire an interior decorator."

"Wouldn't work."

"Ah." She rubbed her hands together. "Am I picking up the real reason you ended up in a godforsaken small town? An affair with an interior decorator?"

"Did anyone ever mention that you were nosy?"

"Just my mother. Come on, give. What good is a secret if you don't tell it?"

"It isn't a secret," he said with exasperation.

"Well, that's great, because then you can tell me the story for sure," she said beguilingly, and made him laugh. More to the point, he gave in.

"I started out in Raleigh, North Carolina. Grew up there. Still have family there. I was engaged once, back when I was still going to be a lawyer, but she didn't like it when I turned blue collar."

"So she was stupid. Thank God you got rid of her," Daisy filled in.

"Um, actually, she got rid of me—"

"Either way, you got saved from a fate worse than death. So. What happened after that?"

"After that, I met up with Jim Farrington—the best carpenter I ever met. I started apprenticing with him. He was obstinate as a mule, but fantastic as far as his work. He had a younger sister."

"Aha."

"Yeah. I guess you could say that was an 'aha.' I took one look at her and fell so hard I'm not sure I ever got up again. I was ready to marry her on the first date, but actually, it made more sense for me to work my way into a partnership with Jim. It takes money to marry, start a life. And she didn't want to settle down that fast, anyway. So we hooked up for a couple years, planned on marrying, just didn't do the deed. That is, the marriage deed—"

"Um, I don't need to hear details about any other kinds of deeds."

"Okay. Anyway, a problem came up."

"And the problem was…?"

"Well…I can't tell you how good a person Jim was. Or how good he was with the work. That's the thing, the whole reason I was sure we could make a great partnership. He felt the same about me. Only for some reason he always thought he was right."

"Was he?"

"Hell, no. I was the one who was always right."

"Ah. I'm beginning to get a much bigger picture now."

"As far as Jim, if he said black, I said blue. If he said right angles, I said left. We started out fighting with each other, but then we started fighting in front of clients, too. If he hadn't been so bullheaded and sure of himself and uncompromising—"

"Like you?"

"That was exactly the problem. We were like identical twins. Anyway, the only answer possible was to sever the relationship. By then I'd already severed the personal stuff with his sister—she was caught between loyalties, and by then, truth to tell, I think we both knew we weren't going any further together. Anyway, it was at that point I took off, because Jim started the business, so he was entitled more than I was to keep on with it. And I wanted to go somewhere where I could work alone. A place that wasn't so big that a partner was going to be required, but where there'd still be definitely enough work to make a decent living."

"Where you didn't have to worry about someone finding out that you were boneheaded and always right and a pain in the butt?"

"I didn't say boneheaded. I said bullheaded."

"There's a difference?"

"Of course there's a—" Teague stopped talking abruptly. When she cocked an eyebrow in question, he raised a finger, asking her to be quiet. She was, unsure what he heard that had caught his attention.

But then she heard it, too.

Silence.

The fire was crackling in the hearth, spitting sparks and wooshing smoke up the chimney. But the ever-present wolf wind had suddenly stopped.

They both tore off for the closest window at the same time, Teague hobbling on his broomstick crutch. Daisy pushed at the drapes to peer out. Neither had been keeping track of time—what difference did it make with the storm? But it was early evening. Dark. And after hours of that incessant wind and blowing, hurling snow, suddenly there was…magic.

The wind had completely died as if it had never been. Moon glowed on a pristine, pure landscape. It looked as if the Pillsbury Dough Boy had been making whipped-cream frosting in mountainous quantities, with fat dollops here and there, mounds higher than buildings in places, and swirls and twirls and soft cups in other places. Moonshine gave the snow a sugar glaze, yet it still looked soft and cushiony. There were no footprints, no lights, no cars or other signs of civilized life marring the beauty yet.

Daisy felt a deep, raw pull inside her. She'd left Vermont. She'd never wanted to come back. She never needed to go through another blizzard in this lifetime…yet she'd forgotten this part of it. The part when the blizzard was over and the whole world turned magical. The part when there was no other beauty like this—and never would be again—because blizzard snowfalls were never the same. The moonlight, the magic, the diamonds in the snow…it was damned impossible not to feel something. An awe. A wonder. A rush of pleasure, just for the sheer beauty of it.

She turned her head, saw Teague looking at her instead of out the window.

"It's just…so special," she said helplessly.

"Yeah, you are," he said lowly, and reached for her.

Four

Okay, okay. Daisy had known for years she was susceptible to magical moments…and magical men. That was precisely how and why she'd turned so cynical. Hard-boiled cynical. More careful around guys than a nun in a chastity belt, in fact.

But Teague didn't play fair. First of all, he'd been making her laugh. And then out of the total blue, he'd suddenly called her special—when God knows no one had seemed to see her that way in a very long time. And then, when he pulled her in his arms…

She melted like warm ice cream. Like an ice cube in sunlight. Like a damn fool woman who didn't have the sense of a goose.

His broom-handle crutch thumped on the carpet when he dropped it. Both his arms went around her then, his hands framing her face to tilt her lips toward his, where he could sip at her mouth and then aim for another deeper drink.

She had to wind her arms around his waist or risk falling. Her hand let go of the open drape in the process, which cut off the cold window draft and sealed them into their shadowy, fire-lit nest at the same time. She didn't know him. He didn't know her. Yet instead of feeling crazy, a little devil whispered in her heart that this was different. It really *was* a moment in time that she'd never have, never feel again.

He tasted so…warm. So hungry. In that instant she just desperately didn't want to lose that feeling. Eleven years of shouldering her private problems alone suddenly eased. She hadn't suddenly lost her mind. She knew she hadn't faced her immediate dragons, and that reality was going to smack her in the teeth very, very soon. But so many years had passed. She'd forgotten what it felt like…to just feel *good* with someone, to feel that excitement with a guy where desire bubbled up between them like a champagne surprise. To feel delight in a man without worrying how much the later cost would be. To feel something that didn't have unwanted secrets attached.

"Whoa," Teague whispered. "Lady, when you turn on…you really turn on."

"I was just going to complain about the same thing with you."

"Um, just to be straight with you…. I wasn't complaining."

"Neither was I." She tilted her head recklessly. "Are we actually going to lose our heads and do this…or are we both going to use some intelligence and slow down?"

"I vote for losing our heads."

"You really want to be reckless and irresponsible?"

"Yeah. Totally yeah." He hesitated. "As soon as I get a condom, anyway."

Something warmed inside her even more than all that hot, combustible sexual heat. It was just…she hadn't planned on liking a man, really liking one, for at least another millennium. But she loved babies, far too much to risk one, and it was rare to find a guy who put babies first the same way. In fact, she liked him so much at that instant that she had to hesitate. "You don't think you're going to regret this? That we're moving way too fast?"

"Of course we're going to regret this. Of course we're moving too fast." He was still aiming for another kiss, and his voice was thicker than honey. "You know damn well it never works out to have sex too soon. It takes over everything."

"I know. And I know better." She found herself staring at his mouth.

"So do I. Believe me, this is your call. Totally. You want to send up a stop sign, we quit, all's fair. Just try to do it within the next minute, okay?"

"What on earth made you think I was going to put up a stop sign?" she asked. He responded with a quick smile, but that was it; he pounced. His lips claimed hers again in one slow, lazy, breath-stealing sonata of a kiss.

They'd been teasing at the heat thing before, but not like this, nothing like this. This was enough heat to melt all the icicles from the blizzard. There seemed more smoke between them than was zooming up the chimney. Dizzying kisses circled her throat, circled her heart. She was used to passion. She liked passion. Too much. She'd always liked that feeling of recklessness, the taste of danger, of being sucked in by a guy so powerful he gave her heartbeat a kick.

Except, it was only and always the scoundrels who put that zing in her pulse.

She couldn't take it anymore. She could accept that she had terrible judgment in men, that she never fell for the guys who were right for her. But she just didn't think she could survive having her heart kicked again. She had to get tougher. She had to stay away from the scoundrels.

Only, something seemed different this time.

The excitement, the danger, the recklessness and urgency—it was all there. Times ten. But this wasn't the kind of man she knew or had ever known.

"Teague," she whispered in a hesitant voice, when Daisy knew she'd never had a hesitant bone in her entire body. But that seemed to be the precise problem. Her body. The body that was slowly, mercilessly turning into shambles.

He'd already pulled her sweater over her head, sent it soaring somewhere in the dark shadows. His big, callused hands slipped in the waistband of her pants, then, lingered long enough to cup her fanny, then slid her black slacks down her thighs to her ankles. Then—possibly because he couldn't keep his weight on his bad ankle any longer—he sank down to the couch. Only he didn't sit down immediately. His mouth trailed down from her breasts to her ribs to her navel, chasing the same path as his hands did on her derriere.

She was wearing underwear. French underwear. Tap pants, ivory with lace. And that's where his mouth stopped traveling. He lingered there, first kissing the lace, then the ivory satin...not kissing bare skin, never kissing bare skin. But the whisper of satin was hardly a barrier.

An embarrassed groan whispered from her throat, the last sound she made. She couldn't seem to keep oxygen going in and out of her lungs. She reached for him, found the muscles in his back bunching and clenching for her touch. His mouth came back to hers, and while his lips clung to hers, held hers intimately, she pushed at his shirt, pushed at his jeans, pushed at his zipper.

At some point they seemed all tangled up, her trying to pull him on top of her on the couch—Teague trying to pull her on top of him. Somehow the couch got abandoned. It was just too hard to find it with her eyes closed and nothing on her mind but touching him and being touched. The scratchy carpet at least cushioned her bare back, and still he kissed her, rubbing his pelvis against her bare tummy now, so she could feel how hard and urgently he wanted her.

The fire suddenly sent a fireworks of sparks up the chimney. A log tumbled to the grate. All this time, they'd been warm enough with the fire, as long as they wore all their clothes, yet now they were both peeled down to near bare flesh—give or take socks—and she was still amply warm.

Hell's bells, she could have swum in the snow and might still need to do that just to cool off. That funny thought surfaced, but it wouldn't stick. It should have stuck. Sex was fun. It made life worthwhile. It made a woman feel alive, feel important, feel her own power. But it shouldn't tear a girl's soul out, should it?

Daisy was no baby about this. She knew life. She couldn't be fooled by fairy tales, not anymore. But damn. This yearning seeping through her, eeking through her, aching through her, was scary and troubling and...compelling.

Teague's eyes suddenly opened, found hers, held hers. "You ready?" he asked her.

"Oh, yes. Ten times yes."

"If we fall off the world, we do it together."

"Yes."

"I don't give a damn about tomorrow. You're mine tonight."

"Yes. And you're mine."

"Ah, hell, yes." And then he thrust inside her, his head thrown back, the pulse in his throat throbbing as hard as hers was. *"Yes."* He thrust again, looked at her. "Oh, yes," he whispered that third time, as if he were finally there, impaled as deeply inside her as any man had been, any man would be or could be.

And then it was just as he said. She tipped off the world. With him. Into him.

She woke up to a nightmare. One instant she'd been burrowed in a cocoon of warmth and safety; the next, there was a frantic thud in her tummy and fear slamming in her pulse.

Her eyes shot wide. Yesterday morning she'd been wakened by a cell phone, and from somewhere in the house the same phone was beeping now. Everything else was a jolt of a surprise, though. Sunlight sneaked through cracks in the curtains. Every light and lamp in the Cunningham house seemed to be turned on. New noises emanated from everywhere—the hum of a refrigerator motor, a radio in another room, the clang of hot water pipes. A man was wrapped around her as if he were the birthday boy and she was his present.

Faster than a blink she realized power had been restored and the blizzard really did seem to be over. But the man spooned around her, protecting her from dragons and darkness and all... There was the nightmare.

Guilt hit her brighter than the daylight. Maybe she'd curled up with Teague that first night, but nothing serious had happened. She could forgive herself a lost moment in time. But last night...

Last night she'd made love with him—a near stranger. She didn't do that. Ever. She was capable of being very foolish, of making impulsive decisions, of choosing the wrong men. But she'd never been a complete and total idiot before.

"That cell phone," the low-whiskey baritone said to the curve of her neck, "keeps ringing. Apparently the caller's not going to give up. You want me to get it?"

"No, I will. You're just going to hurt your ankle if you try to hustle. And it has to the sheriff." It was. Unfortunately, she couldn't discover that for sure until she'd charged out from under the covers naked as a jaybird. The cell phone was in the kitchen, plugged in, but obviously the power hadn't been on long because the connection was scratchy.

"Daisy Campbell, if you hadn't answered soon, I was going to have a heart attack. I thought something happened to the two of you!"

"No, we're both fine, George." She whirled around, searching frantically for something in the torn-up kitchen to cover herself with. The only thing in sight was a scratchy-looking carpenter's apron. Useful for covering up the front of her. Marginally. Sort of. "I just couldn't get to the phone any faster, but we're both all right."

"Good. Plows have been out on the road for a good three hours now. We should be getting into your neck of the country within the next hour. That's the best I can do. You're high on the list, but we had to clear the highways and town before we could head out for the back roads. I take it your patient survived the night?''

Her patient. The one with the head wound and the sprained ankle. The one who'd made love to her mercilessly and tirelessly for most of the night. ''Um, he seems to be less injured than I first thought.''

''Well, that's good. Still, we should be able to get him checked out at the hospital this morning. Now, as far as you getting to your place—''

''The furnace wasn't working at my parents' house. That was why I trekked over to the Cunninghams' to begin with.''

''All right. When I get off the phone with you, I'll…''

George said something else. She had no idea what. She had no idea when she stopped talking and hung up, either, but suddenly Teague seemed to be standing in the doorway, wearing jeans almost zipped up, looking her over quietly, thoroughly.

His carpenter apron was draped over certain strategic spots and it wasn't freezing like before; the furnace had obviously been chugging hot water through the radiators for several hours. Yet feeling Teague's eyes on her made her feel barer than cold.

Everything about him tracked memories from last night. His tousled hair—she remembered riffling her fingers through that thick, wiry hair, dragging him closer to her, demanding more kisses, deeper kisses, more-intimate kisses. She remembered the taste of that narrow mouth and those smooth, seductive lips. She remembered the exact moment she'd put a love bite on his left shoulder. She even remembered his bare feet…yelping when he'd suddenly touched her with those cold toes, and then laughing, laughing just before he'd pressed her into the blankets and taken her down with another kiss.

By night he'd been her lover…but by daylight he was a stranger. A stranger she'd shared more with—more honesty with—than she had with her husband. She didn't know what to make of that, except that there wasn't a man on the planet who unnerved her. Ever. Until now.

To add insult to injury, the son of a gun had looked darn good in the shadows, but man, he looked downright wicked in real light.

Her stomach suddenly skidded down another slippery chasm. Relax, she tried to tell herself. It wasn't love. She'd been foolhardy to sleep with a stranger, but it's not as if she were in love with him.

She could handle a mistake. God knew she'd had a lot of experience making those. But she wasn't sure she could survive falling in love with the wrong man. Not again.

The way he kept standing there, looking at her, she sensed he was thinking about pouncing again. Leaning against the doorjamb, protecting his ankle by leaning on the makeshift cane, he should have looked weak and pitiful, and instead somehow the darn man managed to be making sinful, irresponsible, reprehensible promises with those sleepy eyes.

Worse yet, some idiotic part of her heart loved those promises. Wanted him to pounce. Wanted to be wicked with him all over again. For Pete's sake, you'd think her mind had taken off for the North Pole and refused to come home. She said firmly, "They're going to rescue us in less than an hour."

"Damn."

She wasn't going to smile. She was going to stay tough. "You're going to mind real food? Getting back to your own bed and your own place?"

He stepped forward. "I'm going to mind not being trapped with you tonight. I'd have liked another five or six days with you. Minimum. Trapped together. Just like this."

A new flutter kicked up in her pulse. Not just a sexual-zing flutter, but a downright dangerous, feather flutter. He was beginning to touch that soft place that she never let anyone near. Pound on a wall, what harm could you do? But pound on that soft spot, and a girl could get hurt really badly.

She knew how to be a wall. For damn sure, she knew how to keep her heart from being broken again. "Naw," she said lightly. "Adventure's always fun. But too many days of it, and we'd have run out of condoms—and food—and you'd probably have started to worry that we were getting too attached, developing 'A Relationship' or some crazy thing like that."

"You think I'd worry about that, do you?"

Nothing she said seemed to erase that dangerous gleam in his eye, so she aimed straight for the best defense there was. The truth. "We couldn't last, Teague. But I'm not going to regret last night, and I hope you don't."

"I don't."

She hesitated. She wanted—needed—to be careful, but she didn't want to leave the conversation with him being hurt in any way. She said softly, "Last night, I feel like…we made a memory."

Those steady, intense eyes never left her face. "I like that phrase. Making a memory. Doesn't happen to me often. Not like that."

"Not for me, either. But I'm not going to be in White Hills for long. That's for positive." She smiled briskly. "Sheesh, we've *got* to get dressed. Clock's ticking. We're going to have people knocking at the door in a matter of minutes."

Yet when she moved toward the doorway, he didn't seem inclined to budge. He didn't touch her. Teague didn't seem the kind of guy who'd touch a woman who hadn't specifically invited it. But trying to cover herself with his carpenter's apron suddenly seemed humorously foolish. She hadn't minded his seeing her naked last night. She'd wanted him to. She'd wanted to be naked for him, with him. But this morning her fanny felt as if it was hanging naked in the wind in every sense.

"Daisy...you really dislike White Hills that much?"

He'd asked the question seriously, so she answered in kind. "Actually, I always loved it. At least when my family was here—we were always close. But for me, living in a small town..." She shook her head.

"You find it boring?"

"Not...boring. But I always felt as if I were living in a fishbowl. Everybody knows everybody else's business. If you wore a red dress to a funeral, everyone in a three-county radius would know it. You can't make a mistake. You can't want something different. You can't be...anonymous. You have to fit the mold."

"What's the mold?"

"The mold is...behaving like everyone else behaves. Around here, the most excitement on a Saturday night is watching tractors drive by and the high school football game. Women still hang out their wash. Guys wash their cars on Sunday afternoon. People pay their bills, raise their kids, compete for the coolest Christmas decorations."

"And all that's bad?"

"Not bad. Not bad in any way for most people." She struggled to explain. "My mom used to say that I was the only daughter she misnamed. Daisy. The ordinary flower. When I could never seem to do anything 'ordinary.' I think I came out of the womb wanting to dance until dawn. And there was no one to do that with. Not here."

"You really hated growing up here." He didn't make it sound like a question. Good thing. Because it wasn't.

"Not hated. I love my parents, and my sisters and I were always thick as thieves. And honestly, I liked the town. It just didn't like me," she said frankly, and then grinned. "You won't like me, either, when you get to know me better."

His eyes seemed to pick up a challenging gleam. "You sound very sure of that."

"Oh, I'm dead sure of it. Neighbors used to say I was as restless as a leaf in a high wind. Mamas used to make their teenage boys go inside when I was driving by, just to protect them from the influence of 'that wild Daisy Campbell.'"

"Now you've got me scared," he said dryly.

They both chuckled—and then both hustled to get dressed and get the house back in order before the snowplows arrived.

Daisy knew perfectly well that she hadn't really scared him, but she hoped—from the heart—that she'd gotten through. She wasn't the kind of woman that a nice guy married. Not a nice guy who was into roots and settling down in a house with 2.2 kids and a basketball hoop over the garage and an SUV. She was the kind of woman who a guy wanted to have an adventure with.

Like they'd had.

Last night.

But good guys didn't last—not with her. Whether it was her fault or theirs, Daisy didn't know. Right then it didn't matter. It just mattered that she'd made sure Teague was warned off before either of them could be hurt—particularly because she was going to be stuck in White Hills for a while.

For his sake, and hers, she intended to stay far away from Teague Larson.

Five

―――――

Teague trudged down Main Street. Since the blizzard two weeks ago, there'd been no bad snowstorms, but no temperature melt, either. The sludge and crusty ice were piled so high you could barely find a decent place to park—which is why he'd been stuck walking the last three blocks. Usually he liked winter, but typically by late January, the snow had dirtied up; people were sick of bundling in winter gear; the thrill of Christmas was over and everybody was broke.

Actually, he wasn't. He was making more money than he had time to spend—a totally unjust state of affairs—but blizzards had a way of soliciting business. When people were stuck in their homes, they tended to look around more, see the cracks, hear the groans. He swore half the town had called him, hoping to get a major rehab project going over the winter. More to the point—for him—was that working nonstop the past two weeks had kept his mind off Daisy Campbell.

Sort of.

Hands in his pockets, he passed by Carcutter's Books, then Ruby's Hair Salon. After Ruby's, he crossed the road, automatically bending down to save little Tommie Willis from falling—that kid was always getting away from his mother, and the pavement was extra slick this afternoon. Still, he barely noticed the child or the storefronts.

She was still in White Hills, because everywhere he went—customers, gas station, hardware, grocery store—people were buzzing about the glamorous, prodigal daughter come home. But he'd driven out to the farmhouse countless times. No one was there and no phone had been hooked up.

It wasn't as if he assumed they had a big thing going. He didn't. But she distinctly hadn't called him. It's not as if he were hoping for the earth and the sun. He just wanted to find out if she could possibly, conceivably, want to turn his nights inside out ever again in this century.

The wind whipped around his neck, slapped his cheeks red. That's how his heart felt. Slapped. Obviously he hadn't turned *her* nights inside out. And since he knew he functioned best solo, he had no explanation for his heart feeling so roughed up and skinned.

He hiked on, his ears freezing because he forgot his hat—he always forgot his hat. He was headed for Karen Brown's store, a place called Inner Connections. He'd never been inside the decorating place, never planned to, never wanted to. But he'd taken out a wall in John Cochran's house, and they wanted a bay window, and

Mrs. Cochran was housebound because of some recent surgery and she wanted some swatches.

Teague had no idea what a swatch was, but the interior decorating store—Karen Black, or whoever, did curtains and upholstery stuff—was supposed to have them. Lately he couldn't seem to escape this kind of exasperating problem. All his clients weren't as sweet and frail as Mrs. Cochran, but lots of women wanted decorating ideas to go with their carpentry and rehab projects.

Ask him, the whole thing was dumb. When you had a good-looking window, why cover the thing with a bunch of fabric?

He trudged past the barber shop, then Lamb's Feed Store, then the cleaners. First place on the next block was the Marble Bridge Café. In the spring and summer, the café set Adirondack chairs outside so the locals could sip brew and fight about politics, Vermont-style. Teague wouldn't mind popping in for a fast coffee— and to warm his hands—but he wanted to get this torturous swatch thing over with. Maybe after. Assuming he survived the decorating store. Assuming someone was there who could explain about the swatch thing. Assuming…

He stopped dead, then backed up three paces.

Something was odd. He wasn't sure what snagged his attention, but walking down Main Street was invariably like listening to his own heartbeat. He knew how it was supposed to sound. He knew how it was supposed to look.

The Marble Bridge Café was one of those places that never failed to be predictable. By this time in the afternoon, George'd be sipping free coffee at the counter, his sheriff's hat on the hook inside the door. The place

would smell like something burned, because Harry
Mackay—who'd owned the café for the past forty
years—invariably started talking and forgot what he
was cooking. People didn't come for the food unless
they were desperate, anyway. The café was primarily a
breakfast and lunch place that Harry kept open through
the afternoon because he had nothing better to do. In
the early part of the day, it was a place to hang out, to
fight about politics, to read the paper. It was tradition.
And traditionally, by late January, Harry hadn't taken
down the Christmas lights; tired garlands were sagging
from the windows; and the linoleum was muddy from
people charging in with boots all day.

The garlands and lights were there.

The floor was the color of dirty snow.

The sheriff was sipping free coffee.

Teague couldn't fathom what was different—and
then realized there were people inside. By this time in
the afternoon, the clientele had usually thinned out. Today at least half the booths and tables were occupied.
Maybe Harry had a sale on burned food?

The thought struck his funny bone, but Teague would
still have continued on if he hadn't suddenly spotted a
woman behind the counter. Not Janelle or the other
part-time waitress who worked for Harry. Not anyone
he'd ever seen in the café before. And he immediately
pushed open the door.

Several called out greetings. He answered or nodded,
but he hadn't taken his eyes off the woman. Her back
was to him, but he could still tell that she wasn't a
normal woman—at least not normal by Marble Bridge
Café standards. Her height clocked in around five-seven
and she had glossy dark hair, worn shoulder length, the
kind of hair that swayed when she moved and sifted

colors in the right light. She wasn't wearing jeans and an L.L. Bean sweater, which was the winter indoor uniform in White Hills. Not that he'd know designer clothes if they bit him in the butt, but he guessed the silky blue shirt and slacks cost the moon and then some.

It wasn't remotely a wild outfit, but for White Hills, the cut and fancy lines were always going to draw attention. More to the point, he'd have known that glossy dark hair, that elegant little rump, anywhere.

He was halfway to the counter when she suddenly turned around. The instant she spotted him, the instant their eyes met, she froze. She was carrying a plate of cookies, and someone was talking to her from the kitchen—an open transom window led to the back room—but for a moment she just stood there, looking back at him.

Teague knew hurt pride could affect a guy's imagination, yet he swore he saw a willful rose tint her cheeks, a sweep of yearning shine in her eyes. She looked just plain happy to see him—but anxious, too. Still she stood there. Still she didn't move, as if she'd sucked in a sudden deep breath and just couldn't seem to let it out again.

By then both the sheriff and Harry glanced up. It's not as if anyone had a choice about being a stranger in White Hills.

"Hey, Teague," Harry greeted him. "Rare for you to stop in on an afternoon. You playing hooky?"

"Everybody deserves a vice," he said.

"Hey, Teague."

"Sheriff." He had no reason to know George Webster well, but it was the same with everyone there. They knew of him, or well enough to extend a greeting.

By the time he'd shed his jacket and wasted those

few seconds on hellos, Daisy had disappeared back into the kitchen—whether she had a good reason or just wanted to avoid him, he couldn't guess.

Either way, sitting down gave him a few minutes to analyze the situation. The more he looked around, the more he had the feeling that the Marble Bridge Café had turned into an alternate universe. Instead of smelling like old grease and burned food, scents wafted in the air that could make a guy throw himself on the ground and grovel—like the scent of fresh, warm bread. Blueberry muffins. Pastries. Cookies. Delicate, delectable stuff.

Maybe Harry owned the café and was given credit for feeding people, but he wouldn't know "delectable" if threatened with ptomaine.

But it was seeing Daisy—finding Daisy—that kept stunning Teague. She belonged in that café like a Monet belonged in a hardware store. Boots in Vermont meant, well, boots. But she'd paired the blouse and snug black slacks with high-heeled boots so calf-hide soft they weren't meant to ever walk in harsh weather. Silver glinted from her ears and wrist. A tiny towel had been slung around her waist, apparently auditioning as an apron, but she still looked elegant from the ground up.

Daisy? The town's infamous exotic flower and favorite wild girl, cooking in an aging café? Ms. Five-Hundred-Dollar-Boots Campbell, wearing an apron?

"Cold out there," the sheriff said. It was George's standard conversational opener. Since the town rarely needed law for much of anything, there was no reason George shouldn't hang out here, gaining weight on pastries and shooting the breeze and casting moony eyes at Daisy.

More to the point, he was usually good for information, so Teague tried pumping him. "Well, it's sure warm in here, with a crowd like this. I don't get it— I've never seen this many people in the café since I came to live here. What's going on?"

"Daisy's French baking, that's what's going on. About a week ago, Harry let her wander into the kitchen, and ever since then she's been coming out with stuff nobody ever heard of. And before it's gone, you better be asking for the lavender sponge cake. Trust me, you'll never taste anything like it again. I forget what all else she came up with today. You could try the lavender-custard ice cream."

"Lavender ice cream," Teague echoed.

"I know, I know. Sounds like pansy food. In fact, that's what she says, that there's lavender in it. I swear, though, it doesn't taste like any sissy flower—"

Someone tapped on the sheriff's shoulder, and when he got embroiled in that conversation, Harry hiked over from the cash register. "What can I get you, Teague?"

"I've barely got a minute, but I could sure use a fast coffee. And some..." He was going to ask for a piece of the lavender sponge cake, but he spotted the empty cake platter on the counter. "Just coffee," he said.

Seconds later his hands were snugged around a mug of hair-curling coffee, but Daisy still hadn't shown back up. He could hear her voice in the distance—he assumed she was talking to Jason, Harry's brother and short-order cook—but she didn't come back.

He gulped the coffee, burned his throat, and gulped some more. His mind kept spilling out questions. All the evidence pointed to her working here, but that just seemed impossible. Harry didn't hire extras—the café didn't have enough business to justify more staff, especially in the slow month of January. And Teague couldn't fathom why she'd seek any kind of job, much less a low-paying one, when the clothes she wore cost more than most of the cars parked outside. Besides which, he couldn't figure out what she was still doing here at all, when she'd made such a point of telling him how much she hated small towns.

One other question hammered at his mind. The same tiny question that had been jamming his brain in the wee hours of every damn morning since he met her. If she'd hung around White Hills these past couple of weeks, then why hadn't she given him a call? Why had she been avoiding him?

Harry twisted his considerable beer belly to engage him in more friendly conversation, but by then Teague had stood up, wrestled some change from his pocket and swung away from the counter. Obviously, he couldn't chase her down in front of all these people. He grabbed his jacket and aimed for the door, thinking that now he knew she was here, he'd choose a free time, a quiet place, to corner her. Yet somewhere between the last table and the front door, his boots pivoted around. Instead of leaving, he found himself charging straight down the aisle, past the cash register, past the counter, past the saloon-style double doors that led to the kitchen area. Harry didn't stop him. The sheriff didn't stop him. Hell, nobody dared try to stop him.

He pushed the swinging doors so hard that one banged against the inside wall. *"Daisy!"* he yelled out.

Almost instantly, two heads showed up from around the corner of the freezer room. The small head with the exotic eyes and lush, soft mouth was definitely hers. The big one looked like a twin rendition of Harry— eyebrows bushier than weeds, a tummy that looked like a hot-air balloon, three sprouts of hair straight on top.

Harry's brother disappeared back into the fog of the freezer room.

Daisy stepped out.

Teague wasn't sure what he wanted to say. Something like, "Damn it, woman, I'm not in the habit of having the best sex I ever had in my life and then having my lover disappear as if it never happened." Or "Daisy, why didn't you let me know you were still in town?" Or "Daisy, for God's sake, what are you doing in this café?"

But somehow he sensed vulnerability in those soft, dark eyes. He knew he was crazy. He'd been crazy ever since he made love to her. Daisy was sophisticated and capable of handling herself in any situation—God knew he'd seen her step up in the blizzard, even if she would hate the idea of being labeled resourceful and practical. The point, though, was that imagining vulnerability in her eyes was likely a sign of more lunacy in him, not of anything that was really there.

Still, something went wrong. He managed a scowl and a bellow, but what came out of his mouth was hardly confrontational. "Daisy, do you know what a swatch is?"

"A swatch?" she echoed in confusion.

"Yeah. A swatch. Like a woman needs to do curtains or upholstery or something."

"Oh, like a swatch of fabric?"

"I think so."

"Well, sure," she said.

"Thank God. Can you explain it to me at dinner?"

"Okay," she responded, as if she'd never disappeared from his life and it was no big deal to go to dinner together.

Possibly he was a certifiable lunatic, but that didn't

mean he'd lost the ability to recognize he'd gained ground. "Seven o'clock?" he pressed.

"Okay."

"Where do you want me to pick you up?"

"How about if I meet you right outside the café here?"

There. He'd got that settled. Before she could change her mind—and ignoring all the interested eyes in the restaurant—he charged right back down the aisle and this time, directly outside. The sudden spank of icy wind tried to slap some reality into him, but didn't seem to work. His head was still reeling. Had he imagined it? That wild night? That extraordinary coming together, the connection he'd never felt with anyone else, the jolt of excitement just talking to each other? Was it some fantasy he'd imagined in the stress of a blizzard? Because he'd had no one for so long? Because he'd stopped believing he'd ever find a woman who bamboozled his common sense ever again?

Was Daisy real—or had being knocked out two weeks ago seriously addled his brain?

As if she weren't already anxious-times-ten to be seeing Teague again, she was running late. To add insult to injury, she was just tugging on a cowl-necked sweater when her new cell phone beeped. Impatiently she grabbed it.

"Finally," a feminine voice scolded. "I got your voice mail about having a new phone number, but you didn't say where you *are*. I'm gonna shoot you if you ever do this again!"

Anxious or not anxious, Daisy had to chuckle. Her baby sister sounded so bossy. Camille had been through hell and back over the past couple years, losing her first love and almost losing herself in the aftermath. It had taken a long time—and the love of a terrific guy—to put that strident, bossy confidence back in her voice. "Hey, I called Mom and Dad and you and Violet, to let everyone know my new phone number—"

"But all you did was leave messages, so no one actually had a chance to talk to you! Nobody still knows where you are!"

"Well, I'm here. Home in White Hills. For a little while, anyway." With the cell phone clapped to her ear, she pushed on black Manolo Blahnik shoes, then stuffed a bill in her Kate Spade purse.

"But no one's there! You know Violet closed up the house for the whole winter. And that I'm off with Pete and the boys."

As much as Daisy missed her sister, she shot another glance at her watch and kept hustling, grabbing a hairbrush, then lipstick. "Like it's my fault the family's gallivanting all over the place? For that matter, you're the only one in the family who's totally settled in White Hills, but instead of being around with your new husband and kids—"

"And dogs. And my father-in-law."

"Yeah. You sure know how to do a honeymoon, kid."

"Quit distracting me," Camille chided. "The last I knew you were still in France. Violet and I both knew there was something wrong with Jean-Luc, something serious, but you never once told us what was going on. The next thing I know, I get the message that you have a new cell phone number *and* you're back in the U.S. *and* your last name is suddenly Campbell again."

"Yup," Daisy said, which seemed to cover everything.

"You got a divorce?"

She couldn't answer that question quite so lightly. "Yes. And I'll tell you about it. And Violet. But right now I'm rushed—just please don't say anything to Mom and Dad until I've had the chance to tell you two completely what's going on first, all right?"

"No, it's not all right. First I want to know—"

"Camille, I can't talk now, honestly. I swear I'm not evading a conversation. I'm just plain short on time. And I need more than two seconds to explain what's been happening."

"Okay, but—"

Daisy hung up. It was already ten minutes after seven. Being a few minutes late wasn't criminal, but she'd asked Teague to meet her outside—which meant he was stuck out there on a frigid-cold night. She tugged on a jacket, locked the back door and charged down the stairs.

She'd carefully thought through everything she was wearing, from the St. John's sweater and slacks to using the last of her hoarded Cle Peau makeup. Daisy couldn't imagine Teague remotely caring about designer labels—and right now, he had no idea that all these silly, impractical clothes were all she owned. She'd played the pricey look up, rather than down, to help create a distance between them. She didn't want him to think of her as normal, as conceivably staying in White Hills, or that there was any potential between them.

That was the theory. But she'd also hoped to have more time to plan how to handle this meeting, and instead felt rushed inside and out.

The bottom door opened into the vestibule of the Marble Bridge Café—and then one more door led her out to the street, where a tall, dark-haired man in a sheepskin jacket stomping his feet to keep warm stood. He spun around when he heard the door, then stopped dead when he saw her.

The streetlamp glowed on his ruddy cheeks and snow-dusted hair, but he looked at her with a fierce glow in his eyes. A blister-cold night suddenly warmed. A lonely heart was tempted…or, Daisy corrected herself, a lonely heart would have been tempted by the promise in those wonderful, sexy, warm eyes if she didn't know better.

She wasn't going to repeat the same mistakes. She couldn't possibly have fallen in love at first sight—or first night—not the kind of love that could conceivably work. It didn't matter what her heart told her. Her heart had been dead wrong before.

"You came from inside the café? It looked all closed up and locked down to me. I never thought Harry kept it open past the afternoon hours," he said in confusion.

"You're right, the café's closed. I'm living in the apartment above it."

He glanced up. "I didn't even realize there was an apartment up there." He opened his mouth as if intending to question her further, but then he looked at her again. Really looked. She had the shivery feeling he would like to swallow her up, because his gaze seemed like a vacuum that sucked in every tiny detail and kept it. "You look terrific."

"Why, thank you, kind sir."

"Only, you look too darn terrific for any restaurant this town can offer."

"Trust me," she said wryly, "you can afford me."

She recognized where he was driving—McCutcheon's, the best restaurant in White Hills—and diverted him to a fast-food burger place instead. He looked tired, her one-time lover. Fit and full of hell and more than capable of causing her a great deal of trouble, but still, tired.

"Your head's okay? All recovered from that major bump?" she asked him a few minutes later—while stealing another of his French fries. It was the first time she'd seen him in clothes, she realized. He hadn't been naked the whole time during the blizzard, but when she'd first found him knocked out, he'd been in work duds. Tonight he wore dark cords and a dark sweater with a Nordic pattern. Nothing fancy, still practical, but good clothes that looked more than good on him.

Daisy couldn't name a single item in her wardrobe that qualified as practical, but that didn't mean she couldn't admire someone with traits she didn't have.

"Actually, the sheriff insisted I go to a doctor, and the doctor decided I'd had a concussion. Like this was meaningful, to have a new definition for a headache."

"And the ankle?"

"Aw, that. Not worth mentioning. I've still got it taped, but that's just because I'm a sissy."

"Excuse me." She stood up, her hand slapped over her heart. "We need to broadcast to greater America that a man in the universe just admitted he was a sissy."

He just grinned—and threw a French fry at her.

"So it was sprained, huh?"

"Just a little sprain."

"Even little sprains hurt like a bear."

"You know?"

She nodded. "I fell off a boat one time, hit an ankle. It was one of my more graceful moves."

"Did someone get a photograph? Because I don't believe this story about you not being graceful."

She stopped dipping fries in the ketchup. She knew

charm. All too well. But there wasn't charm in his voice, only honesty, and that gentle, honest compliment put an itch in her heart.

That's all it was, though.

An itch.

The itch was bad. Downright unignorable and unforgettable—but still, no worse than a mosquito bite. She could get past it. What she wasn't sure she could cope with was getting through a more serious conversation, but she sucked in a breath for courage and determined to try. "Teague, you have to be wondering what I was doing in the café—"

"Actually, I was hoping you'd help me with my swatch problem."

Daisy hesitated. She'd thought his swatch question was a joke—Teague's making up an excuse to have dinner with her. She'd been positive that if he found her again, he'd ask for an explanation of why she'd disappeared after the blizzard and made no effort to contact him.

The truth was, she'd wanted to. Fiercely. She'd had to work on it every day, giving herself emotional pep talks, exercising her hard heart muscle—or trying to develop one. She was in no position to take on any guy, much less one in White Hills. She'd fooled herself before, about thinking a man was right for her. She shouldn't make too much of a one-night encounter. It was the blizzard. A wild moment in time. But that's all.

So she'd told herself.

But looking at him now, laughing with him over ketchup and burgers and fries, she knew why she'd really hidden away. She'd been afraid to see him again. Afraid she'd feel like this. Happy. Lifted up. Her hormones all asizzle and her pulse thumping like a puppy's tail, just to be with him. "The swatch?" she echoed.

"Yeah. Would you mind coming with me? Seeing the Cochran house, the project I'm working on?"

"Come with you?" she parroted blankly.

"It's in town. Just three blocks over. I just want to ask your advice. We could be in and out in ten minutes."

She opened her mouth to say no, but that just seemed cowardly and dumb. What possible harm could it do to spend a few more minutes together, especially at some kind of torn-up construction site? "Okay," she said.

Six

Teague railroaded her to the front porch of the Cochran house before she could balk—although she was thinking about it. "Teague, we can't just walk into someone's place."

"We're not going to just walk in." He rapped hard on the door, rang the bell, then stuck in a key and yelled out a yoo-hoo.

"Teague—"

"They know I come in at all hours. They want to get the job done, so they gave me a key. Just hold up for a second so I can tell them you're with me this time."

He bolted up a staircase before she could respond. So she stood there, feeling ill-at-ease in a stranger's house—even if she did know the Cochran name from her childhood—and more restless than a wet cat in a downpour.

Teague was being easy to be with. Too easy. He

hadn't asked why she was living over the café. Why she hadn't contacted him after the blizzard. Surely he was going to ask some difficult questions sooner or later?

He bounded back down the stairs, carrying his jacket this time and making a motion for her to hand over hers. "They're home. They're happy we're here, and they're even happier that I brought someone to give me some advice."

"You're talking about the swatch problem advice?"

"Yeah. Come on, so you can see what I'm doing." He led her through a hall to the back of the stone two-story house. Obviously, the family was living upstairs for now, because the downstairs was too chewed-up to function in. But Daisy sucked in a breath when she saw what he'd been up to.

Even before he switched on a glaring overhead light, she saw the slate walls and white marble fireplace and the shiny dark tiles. It wasn't like any place she'd seen—not corny country, not citified either, but wonderfully unique without being in-your-face elegant.

"They had beige carpeting in here before. Two cramped little rooms. The fireplace was in the same spot, but it was brick, kind of a dirty red color. It seemed to make good sense to use Vermont white marble, then contrast it with slate—you like?"

"I'm not going to give you compliments for being brilliant. They'd go straight to your head," she said.

He chuckled. "Okay. So you like it. But now you can see the problem." He motioned.

On both sides of the fireplace were two huge, new bay windows. The Cochrans' backyard looked over a ravine, with overgrown woods to the west and a meadow drifting off to the east—a meadow Daisy could so easily imagine in springtime, coming in pale green and then turning lush with wildflowers. "Mrs. Cochran doesn't want curtains," she said absently.

"No?"

"I'm assuming that's why she wanted a swatch, because she thinks she's supposed to have some kind of draperies. A 'swatch' is a piece of fabric so she could see different designs, see how the fabric worked in the room. But she doesn't want to cover these windows, Teague. There are no neighbors to see in. The view is part of the beauty of the room." Daisy wandered, touched, looked. "What she's probably more afraid of is that all these new textures could come across as cold. Attractive, but not warm, not like a home."

"Yeah?"

"Yeah. And the truth is that the textures are cold. Beautiful, but cold." She touched the marble fireplace, the slate wall. "The thing she needs to work with, though, is the furniture. No wood, no arms or legs showing. All upholstery. She needs to choose soft fabrics, like ultrasuede or micro fiber. And then colors bright enough to attract the eye—colors with courage. No grays, no colors with gray in the paint. Yellow would warm it up. Or red. Or prints with warm colors. And then she needs a throw rug—just one—round, not rectangular or square. The rug also needs to have some kind of thick texture, like sheepskin or fur or fake fur—something with body and depth…" She could picture it. Her fingers itched to get into the colors, the fabrics, that could make this fabulous room come to life.

"Um, you wouldn't mind telling Mrs. Cochran this stuff, would you?"

Daisy glanced back at him, startled. "I can't imagine

she'd want to listen to a stranger's advice. I was just woolgathering to you.''

"Trust me. This is exactly the stuff she wanted me to tell her. Only, I didn't get it. I understood how to make better use of the space, how to make the view come to life, showcase the fireplace, all that kind of thing. Hell, I love those kinds of problems.''

"And you did fabulously. If this were a room in my house, I'd hang out here and never leave.''

That was obviously too much praise. Whether consciously or unconsciously, he backed away a few steps, looked out at the snow-covered woods. "I like it okay. It isn't my best. Mostly what I like about carpentry is studying someone's house, figuring out what works for what they want, what they need, what would make the most of their specific living space. So each job is individual to the person or couple, you know? Except…''

"Except what?''

"Except that I just can't handle the decorating-stuff part of it.''

The way he shivered in mock horror made her chuckle. "What, you're afraid of curtains? A great big lug like you?''

He turned, pinned her with a look that was suddenly quiet, suddenly intense. His eyes seemed to catch fire. "And what are you scared of, Daisy?''

She didn't immediately answer, simply because she didn't have to. They both heard the clip of footsteps, and then the Cochrans walked in. Introductions followed, and faster than two women could smell a sale, she was sharing decorating ideas with Mrs. Cochran.

It was well over an hour later before they left the house—with the Cochrans still trailing them, coaxing them to stay for another glass of wine.

By then the temperature had fallen a good dozen degrees and snow glistened in the air. She was warm enough, with fur mittens and a fur scarf, but Teague was hunched in his jacket.

"You goof, where's your hat?" she teased him.

"The town's decorated with my hats. I don't like them, so I seem to unconsciously leave them wherever they get tossed."

"You're going to freeze." She hooked her arm with his, snuggling closer. They'd been getting along like brother and sister, she told herself. Teasing. Talking. Just being together. It was only three blocks back to the café.

Unfortunately, it just wasn't long enough to delude herself. She didn't feel like a sister with Teague. He didn't look at her like a brother would. It wasn't working, the pretending, no matter how hard she tried.

When they reached the café, it was closed tighter than a drum. An occasional car dawdled past. Streetlights turned red and green with no one to see. The overhead security light helped her find the key in her purse. She plucked it out, looked at him and then hesitated. "Would you like to come up?" His expression changed so fast, she added swiftly, "Not for the reason you're thinking."

"What, you think I planned to jump your bones the instant we walked in the door?"

"I wasn't worried about you, Teague. I was afraid I might jump you, not the other way around." She could see he liked it, the teasing, but as she led him up the dark stairwell, her heart seemed to be suffering sharp pangs of nerves.

He'd allowed the easy familiarity between them. Hadn't asked her a single question. Hadn't implied in any way that they'd spent one wild, long night naked together, hadn't pushed in any way.

It wasn't natural, a man being that nice. In fact, it was so unnatural it was nerve-racking.

It wasn't that she owed him an explanation of her life or anything else, just because they'd slept together. But there was something about the damn man that made her want to be honest with him. At the top of the stairs she opened the door, but before she flipped on a light, she turned and said seriously, "If you see my place, I think it'll explain a lot. Enough so that you just might not want to jump my bones the way we did before. That was a blizzard. A wild moment in time."

"As compared to this moment, which is…?"

"More like straight old real life." She flipped the light switch. Without looking at him, she slipped off her coat and scarf, tossed her bag on a chair and aimed for the wine. She wasn't trying to create a cozy drink-together atmosphere, but almost anyone could look at her current "home" and need some whiskey to absorb the shock.

Moments later she handed him a glass of Merlot. Not good Merlot. For damn sure, not French Merlot. Just the stuff she'd found in the grocery store—which was even then too expensive. Of course, air was too expensive for her these days.

"What in God's name was this place when you moved in?"

"Some kind of storage attic. Which is undoubtedly why Harry was willing to give it to me rent free," she said dryly.

She watched him look around. He'd shed his jacket, but he hadn't sat down yet, didn't look as if he was necessarily going to.

Her first week here was right after the blizzard—when she'd realized the farmhouse furnace needed a complete overhaul. That wasn't her expense problem. It was Violet's. And Violet could afford it just fine. But it was going to be another three weeks before the plumber could even get to the problem, and by then she'd realized how much it would cost her to live home…and how bad her financial situation really was. That same day she'd seen the Temporary Help Wanted sign in the café window.

This room…well, it had taken her seven days of scrubbing before she could even stand it. Apparently no one had ever washed it before. Mice and birds and bees had set up housekeeping under the eaves, but nothing human. There was a utilitarian bathroom with a teensy shower; the white porcelain sink was rusty, but it was all usable. And there were two windows built into the slant of the roof.

When her boxes had arrived from France at the farmhouse, she sorted through and discovered that she had all kinds of "things." The only thing she didn't have was money.

So there was an original oil over the couch with no springs. The old iron bed was nothing to admire, but the quilt was convent-made, in rich purples and lavenders. She'd covered a hole in the wall with a Versace blouse, draping it as if it were intended to be a wall covering. She'd used scarves—Hermes, Dior, Chanel—to cover the paint-scarred tables. Her china was fine-boned, a pale cream with a rim of gold, even if the rickety card table was the only place to eat. A hot plate and small fridge functioned as her kitchen.

"If I tried to explain this to anyone, they'd never believe it," Teague said.

"Yeah…well, that's my reality. I'm dead broke. And I do mean broke."

"That's not what I meant or thought. You've made something original and interesting and even beautiful out of…out of God knows what."

"It's hardly beautiful."

"Yeah, it is. All the color, the scarves and stuff…it looks intentional. Not like you're covering up the horrible room. But like you were creating an artsy cool boudoir."

She frowned, confused.

"Okay, okay," he said. "You want me to take this more seriously. You're not just broke. You're *really* broke."

"Yes." She hesitated. "Teague, I don't mind you knowing. But I'd appreciate it if you didn't say anything around town, because my parents and family still communicate with a ton of people here. I don't want word to get back to my family. Obviously, they know about the divorce, but not much more—and especially not what financial shape I'm in. It's just…complicated. They didn't know I was unhappy."

Somehow she found herself sitting across from him, Teague on the couch, hunched over, playing with that wineglass, and her settled at the bottom edge of the bed. There was no other place to sit, not where she could comfortably face him. "Why?" he asked bluntly.

"Why what?"

"Why didn't you tell your family how unhappy you were—or that you're this strapped for money?"

"Because." She lifted a hand in a sweeping motion, one of those gestures that was supposed to communicate there were a zillion reasons. "At the time I first realized the marriage wasn't going to make it, my mom and dad were just retiring. I was in another country. They would have worried to death. And I didn't tell my two sisters…''

"Yeah, they're another question. I thought you said you were really close to your sisters."

"We were. We are. But I'm the oldest, you know? I'm the one they always looked to for advice, to take charge." She added, "In fact, I'm the one who did a little masterminding behind the scenes to help them hook up with the guys they just married. Good men. And they're both totally happy—''

Teague didn't exactly interrupt her, but he acted as if he had no interest in hearing how happy the rest of her family was. "I get it," he said. "You didn't want your family to know because of pride."

She scowled. "All right. So I have a little issue with pride."

"Little?"

"Okay. Big." *Cripes,* she'd have denied it if she could. Unfortunately when it came down to it, except for all the designer clothes and accessories, she pretty much didn't have a pot to pee in. And pride or no pride, she felt the oddest sense of relief to finally tell someone. Someone not her family.

And Teague could have judged her. Instead he just seemed to keep taking in information like a sponge. "The point isn't your pride, sweet pea. The point is…where you're going from here."

"Well. Like I told you, I'm living free above the café, because Harry was hot to have someone in the place. Food's free, rent's free, electricity—it isn't costing me a dime to be here. On top of which, I'm a little short on wheels temporarily."

"You had a car," he said with a frown.

"A rental car that I picked up at the airport. And that's the thing. I don't need a car at all for a few weeks if I live here. I can walk anywhere in town and eat downstairs."

"In return for which, Harry hired you on as a cook?"

"Not exactly. Harry said he hasn't got enough business at this time of year to hire anyone full-time. But we made a deal. Most days, I open and close the place for him—which is easy for me to do, living upstairs this way, and that way he can sleep in and leave early. And I'm putting in a few hours—as many as he'll give me— baking. French pastries, fancy stuff. He said he'd give it a try, and even if it's only been a week, it seems to be working to bring in new customers."

"But he can't give you more than part-time hours?"

"No," she admitted. "On the other hand, with zero expenses, I'm putting everything away. It shouldn't be that long before I can put a down payment on a used car. Then I can look at moving somewhere there's some job potential."

"But for right now, you'd like more money?"

She looked at him. That quiet, intense expression— Teague could be very hard to read. Obviously, she wanted more money. She just wasn't sure exactly what he was asking. But before she could even try leaping to a wrong conclusion, he filled in what he was thinking.

"I told you, Daisy. I need help. Exactly the kind of help you could give me. I've got more carpentry work than I know what to do with, but I'm lousy on the decorating end. For a while, when you wanted to, you could work as a consultant. Even better, you could work when you had free time, because the specific hours wouldn't matter to me."

She stiffened. "Trust me. I don't do charity."

"I'm not talking charity."

She pushed off the edge of the bed and started pacing—not that there was more than a few feet potential to pace with. The most walking she could get in was a circle around the couch. "Come on. You told me flat-out that you had trouble working with other people. You said that was how you ended up in White Hills, because you wanted a place where you could make a one-man business work. Trying to do a partnership didn't work out for you, you said. You always want to be boss, you said. You—"

"Yeah, yeah, I know all that stuff I told you. And it's all true. I'm a pain in the butt. Domineering. Single-minded. And it doesn't help that I'm always right."

She had to grin at his arrogance, even if she still couldn't relax enough to quit pacing.

"But this is different," he said.

"Yeah, it's different. Because I admitted being broke right now, so you got the idea I needed a white knight. Only I don't do white knights. And I didn't tell you so you'd feel sorry for me. I'm not having any trouble living poor for a while, so don't waste your breath thinking I need your charity."

"It's not charity I'm offering." Now he was on his feet, pacing, too. There was something strikingly alert in his eyes suddenly—like she shouldn't have mentioned not doing white knights, as if she had once, as if he were taking in that information like a robber learning a bank code. He didn't make anything of that, though. Didn't ask. He just started firmly arguing. "I need help, whether you do or not."

"Sure you do," she said dryly.

"I'm serious. And I told you straight, that I failed playing well with others in the sandbox in pre-K. But

The Silhouette Reader Service™ — Here's how it works:

Accepting your 2 free books and gift places you under no obligation to buy anything. You may keep the books and gift and return the shipping statement marked "cancel." If you do not cancel, about a month later we'll send you 6 additional books and bill you just $3.80 each in the U.S., or $4.47 each in Canada, plus 25¢ shipping and handling per book and applicable taxes if any.* That's the complete price and — compared to cover prices of $4.50 each in the U.S. and $5.25 each in Canada — it's quite a bargain! You may cancel at any time, but if you choose to continue, every month we'll send you 6 more books, which you may either purchase at the discount price or return to us and cancel your subscription.

*Terms and prices subject to change without notice. Sales tax applicable in N.Y. Canadian residents will be charged applicable provincial taxes and GST. Credit or debit balances in a customer's account(s) may be offset by any other outstanding balance owed by or to the customer.

If offer card is missing write to: Silhouette Reader Service, 3010 Walden Ave., P.O. Box 1867, Buffalo NY 14240-1867

NO POSTAGE
NECESSARY
IF MAILED
IN THE
UNITED STATES

BUSINESS REPLY MAIL
FIRST-CLASS MAIL   PERMIT NO. 717-003   BUFFALO, NY

POSTAGE WILL BE PAID BY ADDRESSEE

SILHOUETTE READER SERVICE
3010 WALDEN AVE
PO BOX 1867
BUFFALO NY 14240-9952

GET FREE BOOKS and a FREE GIFT WHEN YOU PLAY THE...

Lucky 7

SLOT MACHINE GAME!

Just scratch off the silver box with a coin. Then check below to see the gifts you get!

YES!

I have scratched off the silver box. Please send me the 2 free Silhouette Desire® books and gift for which I qualify. I understand I am under no obligation to purchase any books, as explained on the back of this card.

326 SDL D353   **225 SDL D36K**

FIRST NAME	LAST NAME

ADDRESS

APT.#	CITY

STATE/PROV.	ZIP/POSTAL CODE

7	7	7	**Worth TWO FREE BOOKS plus a BONUS Mystery Gift!**
🍒	🍒	🍒	**Worth TWO FREE BOOKS!**
♣	♣	♣	**Worth ONE FREE BOOK!**
🔔	🔔	🍒	**TRY AGAIN!**

www.eHarlequin.com

(S-D-12/04)

DETACH AND MAIL CARD TODAY!

our situation's different. I know you're not going to stay in White Hills for long, so it's not as if either of us have preconceptions about a long-term future. And for right now—you don't know anything about carpentry, so you'd have no reason to fight with me about how I do things. And I have no interest in interfering with any ideas you've got about style or decorating whatsoever, so you'd have a free rein. It seems like a workable plan to me. You wouldn't have to be pinned down to a set schedule. You could just work whatever hours you had free.''

Probably because she was looney, it was starting to sound like a good plan to her, too. Of course, she'd fallen prey to persuasive men before, and knew better than to just blindly trust her own judgment. She plunked her wineglass down by the minisink on one of her pacing rounds circling the couch. ''It still won't work. I don't have a car, Teague. How would I get to wherever you were working?''

He plunked down his wineglass, too, which was still full. He really wasn't a wine man. Just like her, though, he seemed to instinctively pace when he was thinking. ''Hmm. Well. I've got both a car and a work truck. I need the work truck.''

''I hear a 'but' in your voice.''

He scowled. ''Because there is one. I do have a spare vehicle. So in principle it'd make sense to let you use it for a while.''

''I still hear that 'but' in your voice.''

''Because it's a Golf GTi.''

She'd never heard of the car, but she knew men and their toys, and he had one of those Guy Looks on his face. ''Ah. Your baby.''

''It's not like an old Jag or anything that expensive.

In fact, I picked her up last year for a song. But as old as she is, she'll still go another seventy thousand miles if I take care of her. And she's the MK 1 version. Cross-spoke BBS aluminum wheels. The golf ball gear lever—''

Daisy cut to the chase, her tone sympathetic. "You just can't let anyone drive her but you."

He didn't immediately respond, probably because both of them were distracted. When Teague put down his wineglass, he'd seemed to forget their pacing pattern and reversed his direction. As a result, they found themselves facing each other in front of the couch—with no passing lane for either of them to get by.

She could have backed up. So could he. But suddenly they were barely inches apart. Close. As physically close as they'd been that wild night of the blizzard. Maybe they were both fully dressed this time, but for her, the same sensations welled up. She felt alone in the universe with just him. No one else in sight or sound.

No one else who mattered.

She saw his hand rise. Saw the fire in his eyes kindle—and then smoke. She knew, inside, that he was going to reach for her even before he did it, and she had ample time to pull away.

Instead her arms swooped around his neck at the same time his wrapped around her waist. His lips met hers halfway.

Ignition was faster than nitro exposed to a match.

She knew he was wrong for her. She just forgot why. In fact, why she was afraid of being with him disappeared faster than a sixteen-year-old with the car keys. Wicked heat seeped from his kiss to hers. Sinful hopes communicated from her tongue to his. Her pelvis so naturally ground provocatively against his groin. He shot up, hard, in the nestling privacy between her hips.

That single kiss darkened, richened. She couldn't see, couldn't think. No matter what he thought, she'd never taken up with a stranger, not like she had that night in the blizzard. No matter what anyone thought, she'd never been the wild girl everyone thought her to be, growing up in White Hills. She'd never even been the wild girl she wanted to be.

Except with him.

Something about Teague—the taste of his kisses, the sneaky stroke of his tongue, the scent of him—set off explosions of bad, bad ideas in her mind. And between her legs.

His mouth lifted…probably because both of them were gasping for breath. His eyes found hers, loved hers, expressed hunger and a fury of frustration…yet his voice was as lazy as a summer morning.

"Okay, okay. You can drive my Golf GTi. But it's a hell of a concession. And don't think I'll just give in every time just because I'm dying from wanting you."

She tried to recoup as fast as he did, tried to laugh, but her legs were shaky and her heart even more so. "Are you trying to suggest that kisses are part of this work deal?"

"Hell, no. I don't make deals about sex. If there's a 'deal' about working together—all I'd say is let's be careful to put all our cards on the table. If an arrangement works for you and me, let's do it. Sex is nothing like that."

"You don't put your cards on the table about sex?"

He raised an eyebrow, managing to look as if he were almost breathing regularly again…even if his pelvis was still rocking against her pelvis. "You know anyone who's completely honest about sex?"

"Yeah. Me," she said.

He chuckled. "Me, too. But the fact is—I don't know how to promise guarantees on something as intricate as two people. From where I stand—I want to sleep with you. In fact, I'd like to have another two-week blizzard where no one could reach you in the entire universe but me. In fact, I'd like to spend the next five years in your bed nonstop. But who knows if that would be a good idea for you."

"Quit making me nervous, Teague."

He stopped smiling. Gently touched the side of her jaw with his thumb. "Somehow I don't think many men have made you nervous. Maybe it's good for you to be nervous. Maybe being thrown off base might be terrific for you."

He wanted her to tease back, Daisy sensed. And she wanted to flirt. Wanted to play the way they'd been playing, wanted to *want* the way she fiercely, wildly wanted him.

But Teague had no way to understand. Being nervous wasn't a joke for her. She simply couldn't let a man throw her off base. Ever again.

Seven

Three days later, Teague hiked toward the café, feeling edgier than a porcupine with an itch.

He'd finished up the Cochran job, had two more projects he was putting in motion this week. Daisy was going with him to see both sites. First, though, they had to settle the wheels thing.

Teague jingled the change in his pocket, thinking that a guy had to draw a line somewhere. Maybe he was crazy to fall in love with her. She was so determined to leave White Hills. So used to the excitement of a more exotic life. So not like him.

Still, he could accept a certain level of lunacy in himself. She was so damned special that he could work with the love problem—maybe—at least a little longer. But letting Daisy drive his car—in snow—was a different problem entirely.

A guy's car could be like letting someone else use

your toothbrush. It was hard. Really, really hard, to let someone else do it. *Really* hard.

He pushed open the door to the café, the knot of dread in his throat feeling glummer by the second. She needed wheels. He had the spare vehicle. It's just…this was not good. To have to test a relationship as fragile as theirs this soon, with something as hairy—for him— as this.

She was free as of one o'clock, she'd told him. It was ten minutes after one right now, yet when he hiked inside, he could see right off that the café was blasting busy…when no place was blasting busy in White Hills in the middle of a snow-crusty winter. Over heads and sounds and smells, he spotted her instantly…talking to some regulars at the bar stools up front, right at the bakery counter. Three guys had her attention corralled.

Her hair was wooshed up today. Clipped somehow. Strands had escaped their prison and were cavorting in wild wisps around her neck. Her cheeks were flushed, as if she'd just pulled dishes from the oven. She didn't look to have an ounce of makeup on, yet her ears were showing off a jewel that matched the same blue-hued stone around her neck. She had some kind of blouse that wrapped around her instead of buttoned, leaving a deep vee for the stone to lie, almost to her cleavage, almost showing her cleavage—only not quite. Even when she was leaning over and the guys were trying their damnedest to get a peek.

"Yeah, you've got that right," she was saying to her trio of drooling fans. "Jean-Luc made it big. He should. He's a really special, talented artist."

"I thought you had to die to make money if you was an artist," one of the guys said.

"Well, he was hauling it in for the last few years. And I can swear on a Bible, he was definitely alive."

The three men laughed. "So why'd you get divorced, then, Daisy? We all thought you had the perfect life. Traveling around the world. Living high and nice and all. Your guy making lots of money. Able to do all the things you dreamed of."

Good question, Teague thought, as he shifted out of his jacket and sidled forward—slowly—because she hadn't spotted him yet. He wanted to hear the answer to that question in the worst way.

It just didn't make sense. If her Jean-Luc was so wealthy, how come Daisy couldn't afford even a used set of wheels? She'd told him a lot the other night...but not a clue what her divorce had been about. He needed to understand how she could have all this expensive stuff, and yet still be the worst kind of broke. Bad broke. No health-insurance broke. Seriously broke.

Smells wafted toward him. The bakery counter had little formal signs now. Lavender Cookies. Brownies with Lavender Whipped Cream. Lemon Loaf Lavandula.

Roast pork with rosemary and lavender had been added to the chalkboard up front—where Harry's lunch specials were usually limited to brats and hot dogs.

And the café had started to look completely different. The grease smell seemed to have disappeared. The cash register shone so hard it looked new. The old red-and-white-checked curtains had been pulled back with ties and the windows washed.

If Harry hadn't been shamed into doing those things in the past thirty years, it was a cinch he wasn't responsible for the improvements—and neither were the two part-time waitresses who'd worked there forever.

So Daisy was transforming the place. The mystery was how a woman who presented herself as willful and spoiled and used to the good life could be such a worker.

Too many customers talking for him to hear everything Daisy said, but as he walked a few feet closer, he picked up some of her comments.

"You're so right, Ted. I *do* love money, and Jean-Luc had a ton of it. But it's like the whole town said when I was a kid, you know? I guess I just wasn't meant to settle down."

"I'll bet you lived in some really fancy places."

"Oh, yes. Aix-en-Provence was one of my favorites. It's a town for artists, with cobblestone streets and fountains all over the place and enchanting little squares. And then there was Bonnieux. There's a hotel there that has the best food I've ever eaten, not just gourmet or gourmand but beyond anything you could dream of...*gâteau au chocolat fondant*...meals served in the garden, with pale-pink tablecloths and flowers. And then of course there was Vence, a mountain town..."

She spotted him, took in a breath and then lifted five fingers in the air. Five minutes? He nodded a no-sweat. He could see that, as lazy as she was talking, she was dishing out confections and swooping away empty plates.

"And then there's the fabulous area around Fragonard and Molinard—that's flower country, and in the spring and summer, they grow lavender, roses, carnations, violets, jasmine.... You wanted another slice of cheesecake, didn't you, Moore?"

A foolish question, Teague thought. Moore wanted anything she dished out in any form.

"Boats, too?"

"Ah, yes. We spent months on different yachts around the Riviera. Jean-Luc was always getting an invitation from..." She sashayed over to him and whispered, "I'm sorry! I didn't mean to be late. But Harry had to pick up something, said he'd be back five minutes ago. I can leave the instant he returns, okay?"

"Totally okay."

He never asked, but she brought him a cookie and mug of fresh almond coffee without ever breaking stride, still keeping up with the guys and their questions and orders at the same time. Teague wondered if any of them remotely realized that she was working. Her slow, lazy voice created pictures of nude beaches and the Riviera and women decked-out in jewels, long yachts and buttery mornings and sun-soaked skin and nothing to do but be rich and indulge oneself.

Ten minutes later she'd hooked a jacket and they escaped. "That was a terrific cookie," he said.

"Nah. Not terrific, but a pretty good recipe. It was the lavender idea that Harry bought into. He was suspicious, but he said he'd try anything to see if he could bring in some customers this time of year. And my sister ran the herb haven for years, so I had an inside to the best lavender source anywhere on the planet."

He stopped her mid street, pulled on her sleeve. Immediately she turned her face up to him—her normal face, her normal voice. Fresh skin, honest eyes, the soft, soft mouth. Striking, yes, even disconcertingly beautiful, but that whole exotic spoiled-woman look had completely disappeared.

He kissed her, just to get a taste. To make sure he was with Daisy and not that confusing woman who'd been weaving those stories in the café.

"Hey," she murmured, when he lifted his head and frowned at her. "What was that about?"

"I didn't want to kiss you," he assured her. "I was just trying to practice being a pickpocket."

"Huh?" She plunged her hands into her jacket pockets. Her right one emerged with a small square box. Inside was a perfect four-leaf clover immersed in clear resin. Her lips parted and then she looked up at him again, this time with more vulnerability in her eyes than he'd seen even when they'd been naked.

"This is for me? You bought this for me?"

"Nope. I didn't buy it." The look on her face was damn near close to his downfall. He knew—from all the evidence—that she was used to all kinds of expensive stuff, so there'd been no point in trying to outbuy what she already had or was used to. In fact, it'd been damn scary trying to think up something to give her at all…but he'd wanted to.

"But then how—hey, you're rushing me along!"

"I know, but we're really getting late now, because first we have to go to my house. Get you familiar with the car. Then you can drive to the Shillings' behind me—"

"Teague. It's beautiful. More than beautiful. It's fresh and different and personal and…perfect."

"Yeah, I liked it, too." He tried to keep up a galloping pace, so she had a hard time keeping up with him, but somehow she still managed to cavort ahead for a second to get a good look at his face.

"You really didn't buy it?"

"Nope."

"Then you *made* it?"

"Are you kidding? No one can make four-leaf clovers."

"I meant the resin. You sealed it in the perfect resin."

"I might have." That was the most he was willing to admit to—at least until he saw how she drove.

The Shillings were expecting him around two, and their house was only a hop-skip from his. But as his white pickup took the curves, she held the four-leaf clover, kept looking at it. And then at him. And then at the road. Hell, had no one ever given her anything that didn't have a price tag attached to it?

"I haven't been on these roads in years," she said quietly. Down Cooper Street, across the creek, came a section everyone called Firefly Hollow. "Does every teenager in the country make out here in the summer like they used to?"

"That was the in spot for kids, huh?"

Obviously, there were no fireflies now, but in the summer the leaves formed a cool, fragrant canopy overhead. In fall the colors were brilliant; in summer fireflies danced in the shady arch. Now it was just a dip in shade and memories. Past the hollow, his white pickup climbed the hill and curved around Swisher's land— Old Man Swisher had a pond.

"Most of the farmers around here have ponds, but his was our swimming spot, because there's a big old cottonwood tree with a limb that was just perfect for swinging into the water."

"So...every single one of your memories of White Hills was bad?"

She lifted her brows. "Good grief, no. It was a great place to grow up. It's just..."

She never got around to finishing that thought. They passed red barns and white fences, hillsides that would be taken over by clover and buttercups in the summer.

Patches of elms and big old sugar maples dotted the landscape, but they were naked now, revealing the underside of their character. Past the red covered bridge, he turned in the first drive.

"Car's in the garage. I've already got the key."

She balked. "What? You mean we're not going to go in?"

"In? Now? We have to be at the Shillings' in a few minutes."

"But you haven't shown me your house." She looked with interest at the white-shuttered stone bungalow.

"We can do that another time." If he didn't get this car thing over with soon, he was too likely to have a heart attack. "You know how to drive a stick shift, don't you?"

"Teague, I grew up on a farm. Of course I can drive a stick. Oooh." When he popped the button on the garage door, she saw his baby. Actually, he figured all she saw was an old car. Someone who didn't know about old Volkswagen Golf GTi's was hardly going to be impressed. But she was a nice shiny black. Waxed to within an inch of her life.

"Isn't she pretty," Daisy raved. "No wonder you're in love with her. What a darling."

He relaxed. A little. "You like her."

"What's not to love. And not a scratch on her."

"Not one," he agreed. Carefully. "You *do* have an active driver's license, right?"

Daisy laughed—right in his face, even if it was a kindly kind of chuckle. And then she motioned to the keys by waggling her fingers in the universal gimme gesture. "We'd better get a test drive over with, Larson, before you have a stroke. Try and stop worrying, okay?

If you can't handle it, you can take back the offer to use your car, no problem.''

"I *want* you to use the car. There are just a couple things you need to know before you take her out." He mentioned a couple of them. Maybe he mentioned a few more than a couple. Hell, who knew how many he brought up? At some point, he realized she was biting her lip, obviously trying to keep from laughing.

"It's not funny," he said testily. "She's got a silky smooth engine, but the Golfs, the original ones, they put the standard drum brakes in the rear. Which means she loves to go, but she's not so excited about stopping. And then her carburetor is a little on the sensitive side—''

"I believe you mentioned that. Twice now. And I'm beginning to get a sneaky feeling how important this car thing really is. If we can survive this—or should I say, if I can survive this driving test—we just might make love again, right? Or else it's all over? Have I got the stakes about right?''

"Well, I wouldn't go *that* far…''

But he was thinking about it. Maybe she'd avoided him, but spending time with her was proving even more tantalizing than before, so now it was impossible not to think about sleeping with her. Making love with her. How much he wanted to, in any form and way she was willing. But before he built any more risky fantasies that they had a shot together, he had to know that she could swallow some of his rough edges.

Teague knew he was good to people—but not necessarily good with people. He never planned on being a loner. By this time in his life, he'd always thought he'd be married, have a kid or three. Instead he'd lost more than one woman—and screwed up a great business partnership—because he had the slight tendency to like things his own way.

He'd told Daisy about some of that. But she hadn't really seen it until the car question came up. The car wasn't the issue. It was just a symbol. And, man, she just didn't know what he had to overcome to let her climb in the driver's seat of his most loyal lover, turn the key, make the engine vroom-vroom way, way, way differently than he did.

"Put your seat belt on, tiger," she said gently.

He clipped his. She clipped hers. Then faster than lightning, she shifted into reverse and they rocketed backward out of the driveway.

Sweat broke out on his forehead.

She took the first curve on all four wheels, but it was close. Then, just past the next curve, he spotted a snow-plow, doddering along around twenty miles an hour. Vermont drivers—it was an unspoken rule in the state—didn't bother using their rearview mirror because they were going to do what they wanted to anyway. Daisy passed the snowplow. On the curve. On the curve with the double-yellow line. Somewhere around fifty.

More jewels of sweat laced the back of his neck. There seemed to be a shortage of oxygen in the car. He couldn't talk. His right foot was mashed on the brake. Except that there wasn't a brake on his side of the car.

"My, she does like speed, doesn't she?"

He spotted a little blue Buick ahead, an older model, the driver in it short with fuzzy white hair, and ahead of her was a Honda Civic. Daisy passed both of them on the next straightaway. The speedometer hit eighty-seven. Not for long. Not even for minutes. But it definitely hit it.

On the next good curvy hill, she practiced down-shifting.

Eventually—long enough that he'd gotten three ulcers—she pulled back in his driveway and gave the brake a good test. "Okay now, tiger," she said cheerfully. "Let's see if we can peel your knuckles off the armrest."

"I'm okay," he said.

"I know you are." She unclipped her seat belt and handed him the key. "Well?"

"Well what?" His lungs were so grateful to be safe that they wanted to do nothing but suck in oxygen.

"Well, did I pass? I know. You undoubtedly thought I'd drive like a prisoner on parole, but I figured I'd better be honest with you. If the car was a test, then it'd better be a true test. Only…"

"Only what?"

"Only what's the verdict? Did I destroy any attraction you ever felt for me? Did you decide there's no chance we'll ever sleep together again, much less that we have any prayer of lasting another day as friends?"

That woke him up. He looked at her. "If you were trying to scare me off wanting to sleep with you, babe, you failed big-time."

"You're okay with my driving?" She lifted her brows.

He was okay with her driving. Just not in his car. Ever again. Yet he heard himself saying, "Sure." As if he were cool. As if the favorite car of his life hadn't just suffered a nerve-shattering risk. As if he wasn't a Type A personality who had to control the important things around him full-time.

"Onto the Shillings'," he said, not wanting to talk anymore. There just seemed no point. Temporarily he was incapable of communicating anything that made sense. His head, and heart, needed time to calm down and cool down. Some good, solid work always did that.

Or it usually did.

They both drove in his truck to the Shillings', because there was no point in using two vehicles to go such a short distance. The plan was for Daisy to pick up the car after seeing the Shillings job. The couple lived on the outskirts of White Hills, in a charming two-story brick house that dated back a good hundred years. Mrs. Shilling, Susan, loved history and tradition, and had loved every minute of fixing the place, until she'd been in a car accident. She'd lost part of one leg. Insurance had enabled them to install an elevator chair so she could get up to the second floor, and for the most part she was functioning, doing the things she loved to do before.

But her kitchen just wasn't working. "The rehab people came over and gave me some suggestions. Also they have a model kitchen at the hospital for people like me, but…"

"But they were generic concepts. Not individual to you," Teague guessed.

"You said it. I want to do the things I want to do in a kitchen. For one thing, it's easier for me to work a wheelchair in here than to hop around, so everything's too high. And their ideas were on relocating supplies, like cans—but I don't use that many cans. I like fresh food. And I like to bake, but I can't get any of my baking supplies from this chair. I can't…sift. Or knead. I can reach the bowls, but then I can't get them at an angle where I can actually work."

"Cleanup's a problem, too?" Daisy asked. Who was

wandering around the kitchen, frowning, analyzing, touching.

"Very much so. I can get to the trash. But I need a workspace where flour doesn't get all over counters and the floor where I have no way to clean it up myself." Susan turned her soft eyes to Teague. "I don't know if there's anything you can do—"

"Oh, he can fix you up perfectly," Daisy assured her.

Teague blinked.

That was the last chance he got a word in. The two women went into a frenzy of "all the things he could do." Pull-out shelves. A pull-out pantry door. Moving the oven down a foot. Create a lower-level, long narrow workspace with rims so nothing could spill from the back and set it on wheels. In fact, Daisy wanted about everything set on wheels.

"Hold your horses, ladies," he interrupted the first chance he could steal a word in. "Susan, we need to talk about what kind of budget you're willing to spend for these changes."

"Oh, money's not a serious problem. I mean, I don't want fourteen-karat-gold faucets or anything ridiculous. But Donald's insisted I get anything I want. He knows how much I love to cook and bake." She was already turning back to Daisy. "You think I could have an extra sink set on wheels?"

"Oh, sure, Teague could do that. No sweat at all."

"Teague can't put a sink on wheels," Teague mentioned. "To begin with, Teague isn't a plumber. Besides which, plumbing takes stationary pipes. You can't just move a sink around—"

They weren't listening to him. A half hour later, though, when they left the house, Susan was as excited as Daisy was. A light snow was drifting down, the sticky kind, that kissed the cheeks and eyelashes and stayed.

"She needs different lighting, too, Teague. Ceiling lights are fine for general light, but—"

She climbed in the truck with him like a born country girl. As soon as she strapped in, he reached over and kissed her. The impulse came from nowhere, yet the result made his pulse teeter and skid. Apparently it ruffled hers, too, because it was the first time she quit talking in well over an hour.

The silence didn't last long, though. "What was that for?" she questioned.

"I don't know. I think it's because you were so gung-ho pushy. Got right in there and took charge. Trouble all the way. I've always liked those qualities in a woman." But he never thought he'd be able to work with someone who was as bullheaded as he was. That he'd had fun over the past hour was still messing with his mind. He added quickly, "But we do need to have a little discussion about what a carpenter can and can't do. I've got a general contractor's license. But I really don't tend to touch plumbing or much electricity. The city and township both have codes."

"Oh. Codes." She said the word as if it were very interesting, she was listening, she cared, and then promptly moved on. "We could make her life totally better. And—if you need the help—I could do more than just the decorating and style side of things. I can hammer a nail straight. And stain. And varnish. And use a drill and saw…well, some saws. I can't use a band saw. But a jig saw or…"

She was still wired up when they reached his house. By then they'd worked up a potential work program— some projects he had to work solo, and his schedule was always wildly different. But he knew he could give her an extra twenty hours a week, if she wanted it. She did. And that set her off on another spill of enthusiasm. In fact, she was still talking when she climbed out of his truck and aimed straight for his back door.

"Whoa," he said. "I thought you had to close up the café? That we were just coming back here so you could collect my car?"

"That was the plan, I know. And I do have to make sure the café's closed up tight by seven. But there's plenty of time before that, and I have to use the bathroom, okay?"

"So you want to see the inside of the house."

She grinned. "You got it."

She shot in the back door and started snooping faster than a bat out of hell. He dropped his mail and keys on the counter, peeled off his jacket, started a kettle.

He suddenly badly wanted a cigarette, but since he'd quit smoking ten years ago, he couldn't do that. A shot of liquor had equal appeal, but no question about Daisy, she was a woman where he needed every wit he had around him.

The same woman who'd waxed poetic at the café about living on yachts and wintering in the Riviera was beside-herself excited at the idea of designing a kitchen for a wheelchair-bound stranger. The same woman who regularly wore cashmere shamelessly boasted about her skill with a jig saw. The same woman who could likely convince a priest she was a spoiled prima donna was up at five, baking for a second-class café in a town she professed to hate.

"You used to have a dog, didn't you?" Her face showed up in the kitchen doorway, disappeared again.

"Yes. Let's not go there." He followed her. The

house—he'd liked it when he bought it. At the time he'd wanted solitude, a place in the country not too close to neighbors, where there was ample space for his dog to roam. At the time he'd accepted being too ornery to ever live with anyone else, so he had no one to please but himself.

The kitchen always seemed okay to him. He used the table for everything but eating—mail, projects, a place to store things he hadn't had time to put away, like Christmas presents from his mother. The sink and counter were both clean. The refrigerator held the important staples—juice, ice cream, ice cream bars, eggs, mustard. He'd sort of forgotten that the kitchen wallpaper was pea green and orange. He was going to replace the wallpaper right after he moved in, but it slipped his mind. Now, though, he could see it through Daisy's eyes.

Not good.

His living room said more for him. At least he thought it did. He searched Daisy's face as she wandered around. The fireplace had a barn-plank mantel, a deep serious hearth. A two-foot brass lion sat at the hearth. No furniture there, just giant pillows, because if you wanted a good fire going, it was because you needed to stretch out and let the fire work on your soul. One step up was the more regular part of the living room, with bookcases and a couch and a theater TV. He had a massive chair—one of those that looked like an upscale lounge chair but actually had a dozen controls.

Daisy took one look at that chair and lunged for it. She sank in, closed her eyes and let out a heartless erotic groan. What controls she didn't immediately find, he pressed for her. The chair was actually a rip-off. It worked; it was just a lot of money for something that he forgot to use most of the time. But watching her bliss out made him think it was worth every dime.

That thought pestered his mind, unsettled him. He was coming to realize that he could look at her—her face, her hands, her knees, or any other part of her— and never seem to get bored. Just looking seemed like chocolate. No matter how good it was, you wanted more. Even if you'd just had a look. Even if you'd just had a taste.

"What's the woodwork in here?" she asked.

"Wild cherry."

"It's gorgeous."

"Yeah." He loved good woods. She already knew that. She was also suddenly bounding out of the chair and streaking for the hall. "Hey," he said.

"So your dog was black and white, right?"

"How'd you know that?"

"Fur in the carpet, on the chairs, on the couch." She turned right, with him trailing her. She poked her head in the bathroom, switched on the light, took a look at the dark-green and white tiles and sink and the puddle of thick, beefy towels on the floor and moved on. "So," Daisy said, "I figured she was spoiled rotten."

"My dog?"

"She was allowed everywhere. Good spare bed-room," she announced after she'd inspected it.

Hell, she was starting to make him so nervous that he started chattering like she did. He used the spare room for an office, but had a couch that made into a double bed for when his parents or younger sister came to visit. He'd built the screen to hide the desk and file cabinet and computer then, to make it more a decent retreat for company. And that room had its own small bath. No towels on the floor. No toothpaste in the sink.

"Where's the wild cherry wood come from?"

"Georgia. Maybe you don't want to look down there."

"Don't worry. I've seen unmade beds before." She smiled before opening the door to his bedroom. He'd built the frame to put the king-size mattress on, because his back could get tricky, and he needed a hard mattress. The double-down comforter was the opposite, all soft and fluffy and embarrassingly sissy—but hell, Vermont winters were damned cold. Especially when a guy was sleeping alone.

Because he was suddenly nervous—hell, he was *never* nervous—he seemed to be bumbling on again. "Look, I know the dresser looks messy, but I swear, things climb up on that dresser in the middle of the night. I can't explain it. Like that hammer—I never put it there. And the fork. I don't eat in this room, so I have no clue how that fork showed up. And all those socks. I never left a sock lying there in my entire life—"

She chuckled. "I believe you. Completely," she assured him.

"Good."

"She was a girl, wasn't she?"

"Who?" He hadn't had a woman around in so long that he couldn't fathom what Daisy could be leaping to conclusions about.

"Your dog," she said gently, and motioned to the pink dog collar on the dresser along with all the rest of the debris. "Aw, Teague. You lost her recently, didn't you? And you loved her a ton."

"She was just a mutt."

"Big deal. You still loved her beyond life. She

owned the whole house, for Pete's sake. It's obvious.'' Her voice was softer than sunlight, gentler than compassion.

Did he need this? Like a hole in the head he needed this. She could have commented on his messes and his ugly kitchen wallpaper. She could have teased him about the towels on the floor. Instead…*damn,* but he'd loved that dog.

''What was her name?''

He'd called her Hussy. Which she wasn't. She never left him, went with him to work anyplace they could tolerate dogs, never got in his way. ''I wasn't looking to have a dog. I just came across her in a ditch one day. Some car had hit her.'' She'd been just a puppy, bleeding, bewildered, too close to dying to even whine. She never did have much of a voice. Worthless as a watch dog. The only one she ever watched over was him.

''Aw, damn, Teague,'' she said softly. ''I'm sorry. That's rough.''

How the hell had she found out his weak spot, just like that, just walked in and in one look, found the one thing he didn't want her to find.

''You know,'' he said, hearing the frustration in his tone, ''it's about time you owned up to a few things.''

''Like what?''

''Like what it's all about. Making people think your ex-husband was some kind of jewel. Rich. Famous. Fascinating. But you're here, Daisy, and you're struggling to get even some basic security together. I understand about pride. But I don't get why you're keeping what happened such a secret. Not from people who care about you.''

He didn't mean to pry. He figured he'd find out in time. What good did prying ever do? People shared when they were ready. If you pushed them, it never came out the same way. You never found out when they were ready, for one thing. But Daisy...she'd made him think about Hussy. She'd poked. She'd looked at him with those loving, caring, beautiful dark eyes.

She still was. And suddenly she was walking toward him, as well. He thought she intended to leave the bedroom, and he turned sideways to give her room to pass.

Only, when she reached his side, in the shadow of the door, she faced him. "I'll tell you about Jean-Luc if you want to know," she said. "But not now. There's only one thing on my mind right now."

"And that is...?"

"You, tiger. Just you. Only you." And she reached up, and lassoed her arms around his neck.

Eight

He wasn't expecting the kiss, Daisy knew. He was exasperated with her. She knew that, too.

But she didn't throw her arms around him because she *wanted* to. For damn sure, she would never have done an eyes-closed, mouth-open kiss-from-the-heart if she'd had any—*any*—other choice.

"Dais—"

"Shh!" she ordered him and resolved not to let him up for air ever again. Or at least for a while. A long while. She back-walked him down the hall, past the living room and den and bath. She walked, blind, her arms slung around his neck, fingers shivering in his scalp, lips clinging as if she were the glue and he was her only stamp.

Anxiety nipped at her conscience. This was such a bad idea—in principle. After the blizzard, she'd steered clear of Teague for an excellent reason. She knew she was vulnerable to him, and she wasn't climbing into another relationship that couldn't work out. If a woman quit trying to climb mountains, then she couldn't fall off.

But damn Teague. *Damn, damn, damn* Teague. She kissed him again, harder, softer, deeper, wilder, loosening her arms from his neck so she could pull at his shirt. And once she'd peeled loose his shirt buttons, she yanked off her sweater—although the instant her mouth lifted from his, he tried to say, "Daisy—" again.

"Shh." She had his bare chest now. She'd uncovered these treasures before. The slope of his shoulders. His upper arms, muscled as hard as sailor's rope. Patches of chest hair, not soft, but as wiry as his temperament was. And an Adam's apple that was throbbing, throbbing, for the lick of her tongue.

It was his fault—because of the dog. He'd broken her heart, seeing how much he'd obviously loved his dog. Teague sounded so tough, but she'd seen the collar, the pink-stuffed teddy bear with the eaten-off nose. The pink tennis balls peeking under the couches and chairs in the living room. The ceramic feeding bowl with Hussy engraved on it, clean, sitting on the counter, no food in it but somehow he hadn't been able to face putting it away yet.

She was so touched, he'd almost made her cry. Made her afraid she might cry. Losing his dog had so clearly devastated him, and all for a mutt.

Obviously she had to kiss him.

And kiss him good.

In fact, as far as Daisy was concerned, she had no choice about making love with him, either.

And making love *right*.

"Um, Dais—" He didn't seem to mind her unbuttoning his jeans, but his big callused hands suddenly, softly, framed her face. "I don't know what pushed your on button—"

"You did."

"Uh-huh. Well. I'm glad I did. But I could have sworn you said you had to be at the café—"

"I do. Later. We might have to hurry."

"That, um, won't be a problem. You want speed, trust me, I can give you speed. But—"

"No buts, tiger." She lifted her head, eyes suddenly stricken. "Unless you don't want to make love?"

"Trust me. I want this. I want you. Full-time, part-time, fast, slow. Any way you're willing to do this." While she had her hands on his jeans zipper, he handily slipped both his hands down her spine, down her back into the waistband of her pants. Somehow he started pushing her pants down at the same time he caressed her fanny, kneading and squeezing. His mouth was leveling hers at the same time.

Daisy intended to protest. *She* was the one in charge here, not Teague. She was going to remind him about that…in just a minute or two. Her slacks were trying to trip her. She stepped out of them. And while she was attempting to step out of them, Teague took the opportunity to lift her high—high enough to tongue-tease both her nipples, first one, then the other, taking his time…my, the man was strong…before lowering her onto his platform bed. Who knew they'd even made it all the distance to his bedroom?

It was downright impossible to get his jeans off when he was on top of her, but she was highly motivated…groaning under his weight, moaning under his touch, demanding more of both. His bed was another reason she'd felt forced into this drastic behavior choice. His whole house was so pure guy. The wood. The stone. A jar of mustard sat all by its lonesome on its own shelf in the fridge. His chest of drawers had a fork and a hammer and a tower of books and socks. His mattress was harder than concrete.

But then she'd seen that hedonist, floofy, fluffy comforter. And now she could feel it, soft against her naked skin, cushiony so that she felt she were sinking, sinking into a cloud…or maybe that was sinking into Teague. An ardent, wild Teague, who seemed to forget time, place, and the phone ringing somewhere in his house.

The comforter and dog were the only soft spots in Teague she'd found. The only hints that he was lonely. That he had needs. Wants. That he yearned…

And damn, so did she. He'd broken her down. It's the only way she could think of it. She'd tried so hard to be mean. She'd tried to scare him, by driving his car in a way that had to turn him off. She'd barged in his business with his customer. She hadn't come clean with him. And still he was good to her. Still, he seemed to want her.

Still, he touched her in ways—deeper, more worrisome ways—than any man ever had.

Those jeans of his—she finally won them. And one of his socks. The shadows in his bedroom seemed darker than smoke, yet there was nothing but searing bright sensations running through her. Greedily she touched, wooed, claimed. Her blood raced hotter and faster because of how fiercely he responded to anything she did. He just kept giving and giving and giving.

She reared her head up, eyes glazed and crazy with wanting. "Teague—I don't love you," she whispered urgently.

His mouth was wet from her kisses, his eyes as glazed and dark as her own, yet he responded easily, as if he were expecting the comment. "You think not?"

"All right. Maybe I do. But that's just about loving you right *now*. It's because these moments together are so good, so right. But it doesn't mean ties or future or permanence or anything like that."

"I know. You're leaving town."

"Yes."

"As soon as you possibly can."

"Yes."

"So this is ideal, isn't it? Exactly what you want. We can make love and make love and make love. And you can forget me as soon as you're gone."

She was about to say yes again, only that wasn't what she'd said or even meant. She frowned, and then the chance to answer him disappeared. He swooped her around, pinned her beneath him, and in the darkening shadows pounced. Kisses dropped on her throat, between her breasts, on her navel, then on the swell of her abdomen. He was aiming…the wrong way.

She was going to tell him about that, mention that he'd lost his sense of direction entirely, except that he wrapped his arms around her thighs, pulling them up even as his head dipped down. All that urgent rushing, yet suddenly he moved slow. Slower than honey. Slower than shadows on a summer night. His cheek nuzzled the inside of her thighs. She felt his rough beard, felt his breath…lost her own.

Her sisters whispered about this. Women were supposed to love it. Not her. It always made her feel too vulnerable, too…naked. She was all about being wild, always had been, but not like this. Not. Like. This. It was uncomfortable and upsetting and…

"Sheesh, Dais, I'll never stop if you respond like that. Come for me, love. Come. Give in, let it happen." He wasn't talking, wasn't whispering. It was a croon to her, a promise.

"I don't...I can't..."

He chuckled, a soft earthy sound, a vibration low in his throat that he transferred to a kiss on that most intimate part of her. "Okay, then. Fight it. It'll be fun."

It wasn't fun. She felt need tear through her like fire, burning, flames licking at her consciousness, blinding sharp. She tried to hold back. Tried to hide, but desire kept escalating, scaling that mountain of hungry, greedy need...until she tipped over the edge and soared.

He took his own good time about shifting, finally came up to smile wickedly at her in the darkness. "You'll be sorry you showed me how much you liked that," he promised. "You'd better believe I'll remember the next time."

She couldn't answer him. He didn't seem inclined to give her a chance to, anyway. He lifted her legs high and tight around his waist and then dove in, drove in, all at once. She felt a yielding of loneliness inside her, a keening to be like this, with him, forever, like this, but of course that was just her heart talking. How was she supposed to think? He was thick and hard. He was whispering wicked ideas to her. He was holding her, holding her, so she couldn't escape yet another climb toward release, every muscle in her body straining for the next cliff edge, the next mountain top, and then there it was...another sensation, like flying free, flying through a silver wind, a flashing-soft sky, soaring...straight back into his arms.

"Oh, yeah," he whispered exultantly, as if this were what he expected all along. As if he always made the world tilt when he made love. As if he always turned a woman into shambles when he made love.

As if he loved her.

Eventually she started breathing again. Eventually she even opened her eyes. She seemed to be wrapped around Teague's naked body tighter than a present at Christmas, both of them smelling like sweat and sex, neither of them moving.

She wanted to move. She wanted to lift her head and stare at him. It's not as if she hadn't been married. It's not as if she didn't enjoy sex. But Teague…they'd made love in the blizzard, and she'd been so sure that was just a lost moment in time. Now she wanted to know where he got his Wheaties. Where he learned all that wicked stuff. How come he moved her to heights she'd never climbed before.

But she didn't look at him, didn't ask him. For just a moment more, she wanted to be nowhere else but right here, snugged in his arms, no reality intruding in any way.

But, of course, there was no escaping reality. An alarm clock ticked right next to her head. "I have to go. Close up the café."

"Yeah, you do. But first you promised you'd tell me about your ex."

"Now?"

A low chuckle came out of his throat. "Hey, you think I want to talk about another guy after we just made love? On the other hand, I don't often have you naked and vulnerable. I figure I have to use this to my advantage while I can."

"Idiot," she murmured affectionately. He had to know that he wasn't being manipulative at all, not when he told her exactly what he was doing. "I told you I'd tell you—"

"Yeah. So spill. Exactly why you're so poor if your ex is supposedly so rich and successful. Exactly why didn't you want your family to help you or know how much trouble you were in. Exactly why you got the divorce."

"Sheesh. Could we work on one question at a time, tiger?"

"No. All at once. Let's just get this conversation over with."

She sighed, staring blindly at the moonlight shining in his bare windows. Rime decorated the panes in magical shapes, crystals and diamonds and jewels. The kind of diamonds you couldn't touch, of course—the kind of diamonds that disappeared if you tried to touch them. She'd tried to touch the wrong kind of diamonds her whole life, but how could she explain that to Teague? "I don't know where to start, except that…I always had a panic attack at the idea of being ordinary."

"Since we're pretty short on time, you don't have to waste it telling me stuff I know."

He forced her to grin. "I mean, a *real* panic attack, Teague. Maybe it started from being the only one in the family with the totally ordinary name. I swear I remember fighting it even way back in my sandbox days. I wanted to be different from everyone else. I wanted to see the world. Take big risks. Have a big life. Do exotic, romantic, wonderful things."

"Yeah, so?"

"So, I thought I found it all in Jean-Luc. I thought he was exotic and romantic and wonderful."

"And was he?"

"Oh, yeah. I remember the first time he sold a painting for big money—over a hundred thousand. He rented a yacht. With crew. We sailed with some friends, feasted for four days. He bought me a Hermes bag.''

''I don't know about the bag, but the rest sounds romantic and generous and all.''

''Yup. Only, by the time we got back home, he'd spent every dime. We didn't have money to pay the rent, much less to buy groceries. The car had already been repossessed. Not for the first time.'' She turned her head. ''Suddenly you're real quiet. You getting the picture? Because that's just the tip of the iceberg.''

''Not good.''

''Not good,'' she echoed dryly. ''All the trunks that I shipped home were loaded with stuff. Stuff I could sell, but I just wouldn't get much for it. I mean, it's not like a Natori bra can be resold. And I've still got a few drops of LaMer moisturizer—the kind that goes for a thousand an ounce—but I can't sell that. What it all amounts to is that I'm wearing good clothes because it's what I have, not because I'm trying to impress anyone.''

''But you do care that people think you're successful,'' Teague said quietly.

She didn't answer that. He already knew she had more pride than brains. Besides, he wanted the whole story—and she wanted to get it over with. ''I sold plenty through the marriage. I sold yellow diamonds, black pearls from Polynesia. I've also washed dishes in a bar to pay the rent, and I've cleaned up messes after parties that you just couldn't imagine. When Jean-Luc had money, he loved sharing it with the whole world. No one ever said he wasn't generous.''

''He sounds as practical as a tree stump.''

Again she had to smile. His fingers were sieving

through her hair, creating that light tickle sensation that made her want to curl up close—when she was already as close as a woman could get. "Yeah—and what kills me was that I never wanted to be the practical one. I wanted to be the wild, impulsive one. Everyone in White Hills knew I was born to be wild."

"You are wild, babe."

She closed her eyes, all too aware that she'd completely changed from the woman she once was. The woman she'd once wanted to be. And she still had to finish the story for Teague. "Jean-Luc was honestly a creative man, a talented artist who deserved all the glory he got. But he needs a harem to take care of him. At least three maids, then someone to work and actually bring in food and rent. And then a bodyguard to keep all comers away who'll ask him for money—because for damn sure he'll give it away."

"Sounds like hell to live with."

She whispered, "He was." And suddenly she found it was easy to get out of bed. She wanted her clothes on. Wanted that reality she'd wanted to disappear minutes before. Didn't want to look at Teague anymore at all if she could help it. At least until she had a better handle on control. For some stupid reason, she felt like crying.

"You stayed for so long because you loved him?"

She wasn't a Vermonter for nothing. Her voice was as brisk as a sturdy wind. "Nope. I was wildly in love with him in the beginning, no question about that. But I think love started dying the first day I woke up hungry. I mean, seriously hungry. The thing was, we moved around so much that I couldn't work—day-by-day jobs, sure, but nothing that could have given us some financial stability. We were all over the place. Living with friends one day, renting a cottage or a villa the next—wherever the spirit of painting took him. So…''

"So?" he prodded her when she didn't immediately finish her thought.

In the dark, though, it was hard to find every sock and button…and somehow she didn't want to turn around until she was fully dressed. "So…he gave me the yellow diamond one day—and we had to pawn it the next. That was the turning point for me. I didn't give a hoot about the stone. It was just that I finally realized he wasn't being impulsive and absentminded and a devil-may-care artist. He *knew* we couldn't afford his grandiose gestures. He *knew* they were going to turn off the electricity. He just thought he could snow me, like he'd snowed me all the other times. He thought I'd be swayed into staying by the romance of the extravagant present. He loved me the same way. Hugely one day—and pawning me off the next.''

Teague still hadn't moved from the bed. "Yet you stayed with him for a long time.''

"Yeah. Out of idiotic misplaced pride.'' She lifted her hands in one of the Gallic gestures she'd picked up in that ghastly marriage. "I was just so ashamed to tell anyone. My family thought I had this jet-setting fabulous life. My sisters thought of me as a role model, the one they could always turn to for advice, to take charge. They were proud of me, for living my life my own way, for making it unconventionally. I knew famous people. I dressed in designer duds. I was traveling, seeing the world. Teague?''

"What?''

"I stole a loaf of bread one day.'' She pushed a hand through her hair. "I was hungry. But I wasn't that hungry. And I can still remember thinking, how ashamed my mom and dad would have been if they'd known."

"Well, hell. Let's get a rope and hang you right now." For a man who'd been so somnolently still, he suddenly bounded out of bed in one swift move and crossed the room stark naked. Suddenly he was an inch from her, his knuckles lifting her chin. Before she could breathe, his mouth came down on hers, soft, warm, firm. "I think you can probably let that guilt go," he murmured.

"You're making light of it. And maybe it was just a loaf of bread. But I wasn't raised to take anything from anyone. I still don't understand what made me do it."

"You think you might have felt just a little bit desperate at how you were living? Not knowing where the next dime—or franc—was coming from? That sometimes scared people do scared things?"

"That's not an excuse." But she searched his eyes in the dark room, still felt the warmth of his kiss, of his body, of all they'd shared naked moments before. "I don't know why I'm telling you all this." He didn't answer, just stood there, his finger idly tracing her jawline. "I think I'm just trying to explain...why I kept it all from my family. From the people who knew me growing up."

"You wanted them to think you lived a romantic, exciting life."

"It sounds pretty shallow when you put it that way. I just mean...I hate coming home with my tail between my legs. I hate people thinking I'm a failure. Thinking that I was always a wild, irresponsible screw-up and the life I got was payback."

He stood at the front window long after she'd left—taking his sacred Golf GTi—and he heard her moving to third gear before she'd reached the end of the road and the first stop sign.

His head was buzzing. He'd never dreamed, from the image she put on, that her ex had been such a selfish self-centered bastard. It changed things.

All this time he'd believed her about not wanting to stay in White Hills. Now he wasn't so sure. She had plenty of pluck. She'd coped with a blizzard, coped broke, coped with a selfish liability like Jean-Luc for years. When it came down to it, she seemed to be inspired by adversity, not afraid of it. She'd pushed up her sleeves and become a cook. Made that horrible attic room into something artistic and personal and fun.

He got it. That she wanted people to think she wasn't practical and responsible. She wanted people to think she was exotic and fun and romantic and wild. He didn't understand it, but he did understand that the key to Daisy was her pride.

She said she was proud, but as far as Teague could tell, it was her pride that had taken a battering over the last years. In her own way, on her own terms, she needed to feel that fierce sense of pride again. Not fake pride. Not lying-to-everyone pride. But the kind of pride that made her feel good about herself inside.

She wanted to feel wild. She didn't want to be ordinary. The more Teague repeated those concepts in his mind, the more a plan slowly started brewing. Possibly a goofy plan—but then any plan was better than desperation. Teague understood that Daisy intended to be gone as fast as she saved a down payment on a car and enough savings to take off. And that meant, if he had any way to influence her feelings, he had to move damn fast.

Because he was afraid he'd fallen. Hard and fast. He

already knew the odds were against both of them—but a man didn't feel this power of love very often, if ever, in a lifetime. He wasn't throwing away a treasure if there was any chance he could woo Daisy into seeing herself as unique and wonderful and loving as he saw her.

Nine

Daisy had never spent much time thinking about Valentine's Day, yet for the last week, she couldn't get it off her mind. She wanted to give Teague a present. She didn't have much money, but the present she wanted to give him wasn't an issue of cost. She just had to prowl the market for exactly the right item, and Valentine's Day was coming up in another week so it would give her an excuse to give it to him.

This morning she was standing in the café kitchen with a hot mug of coffee in one hand and a wooden spoon in another, when panic hit.

It was so natural, thinking of Teague as her lover. Thinking of giving her lover a gift. Thinking of the kind of gift that really, really mattered to him—even if he didn't know it yet.

The feeling of panic lunged at her like a surprise nightmare. Holy cow. When had it happened? How could she have done such a damn fool thing as fall completely in love with him?

The oven buzzed, forcing her attention back to practical priorities. It was still ink-black outside, sleet coming down on a day doomed to be gray, as she swiftly took a cake from the oven and then hustled to the counter, where she was tossing together a blend of dried lavender buds, orange zest, and some beautiful baby white onions. Because she was working this afternoon with Teague, she'd come in the café before dawn, hoping to get a bunch of cooking and baking done.

She spun around and reached in the refrigerator for a weighty package of ground round, when her mind did it to her again. Whispered that *love* word.

Her heart started mainlining more panic. Okay, okay. Making love with Teague had been stupendous. More than stupendous. Maybe she found it crazily easy to be honest with him, to share things with him she told no one else. Maybe she loved working with him, pushing him, being with him.

But that was no excuse for starting to believe they could have a future. She knew better. He was as happy in White Hills as a cat in sunlight, when she couldn't possibly stay here. Yet now she realized how long this ghastly problem had been going on. Every time she thought of him, she'd been doing goofy things. Singing out loud. Walking with a little rock and roll in her hips. Thinking of jokes to tell him. Thinking of giving him something important. Laughing for any excuse. Finding something gorgeous in a gray February day that no one could love.

She *had* to get a grip.

"Oh, God. What are you making *now?*" Harry always showed up at the café before sunrise, made coffee and then promptly disappeared into a booth with his paper—but he usually paid no attention to anything she was doing.

She grinned at his suspicious expression. "I'm making *bitoque* with the ground round, *cher*. I told you. I just put a couple new things on the lunch menu. I promise they'll fly."

"I know everybody loves the pastries. But nobody around here wants fancy food." ·

"Now, Harry, how many people showed up here for lunch yesterday?" She didn't waste time waiting for him to answer. "Jason thought it was a great idea."

"He said so?" Harry asked, obviously taking his brother's okay as reassurance.

"He sure did." Actually, Jason had just said, "Whatever." Neither of them had ever varied the lunch menu from brats in a decade, but then, Jason wasn't the most inventive short-order cook on the planet. "I'll tell you a secret, Harry. *Bitoque* is just hamburger, French style. Same old hamburger. Just with a little bit of sour cream, a little bit of consommé, a little bit of secrets. Just enough to make it special."

"All right, but then what's this other thing?" Harry pushed in his stomach so he could find the space to ease in next to her, still looking suspicious.

"Just chicken."

"That isn't *just* chicken. Chicken is a coupla legs, a coupla breasts, then throw it on the grill."

"Jason *is* going to throw this on the grill. It's just going to chill until lunch in this little marinade. Everyone will love it, I promise. Try not to worry." She pulled out two long sheets of plastic wrap to seal the bowls, then impatiently motioned her boss aside so she could put them in the fridge. When she stood back up, he was standing in the narrow opening with that gruff, exasperated look that had everyone else fooled.

"I am worried. About you. You're young. You're beautiful. You're dressed—" he motioned to her Versace silk blouse and navy slacks "—like a million dollars. Yet you're cooking in my café. I don't get what's going on here."

"But I told you what's going on, Harry. I've been cooking for you because I love to. It's always been a hobby, and I haven't had a chance to do it in years, and what fun would it be to cook for myself?"

"Yeah, yeah, I heard all your malarkey." A phone rang from the back office. Harry cocked his head toward the sound. "Go. I know it's for you."

The chance of the call being for her was one in a zillion, but Daisy swiftly wiped the flour off her hands with a linen towel and hustled. It's not that Teague had never called her here, but he generally used her cell phone. Harry just liked her to answer the phone because she played bodyguard for his unwanted calls—particularly from his ex-wife.

The closest phone was in his office—which hadn't seen a dust rag or vacuum in this century, possibly longer. She grabbed the receiver and started to say Marble Bridge Café, but her sister never waited to hear her voice.

"Oh, Daisy. It's me. I was going to wait to call you until a reasonable hour, but I couldn't sleep anyway and I had to tell you. I had an ultrasound. It's a girl."

"Oh, baby." She'd talked to her mom and Camille over the past couple weeks, but she'd only been able to catch Violet when both of them were on the run. Just hearing her sister's voice brought a smile. Clamping the receiver to her ear, she wandered back to the kitchen.

She couldn't cook one-handed, but there were always dishes to rinse, bowls to put away. "I'm so thrilled for you. Are you still feeling good?"

"Better than good. I'm fat as a slug, but I don't care. I'm just so *happy*. It's scary."

"Don't be scared. You deserve happiness." She could hear Violet sniffing, and though it was crazy, she almost started sniffing herself. Margaux and Violet were the emotional ones in the family. She'd taken after Dad, could hide her feelings like a pro, but damn. For years Violet had believed she was infertile. She and Cameron talked about the coming baby as if it were a priceless treasure—which, of course, it was. "You're taking good care of yourself?"

"Hey, this is me. You know I eat right. How's the cooking going?"

"Fabulous. I'm having a ball. I've been using your lavender right and left. Made every recipe Mom ever taught us. Hey, you, we have to schedule a baby shower—"

"Oh, yeah, I'm all about it. But not quite yet. And in the meantime..." Violet cleared her throat. "Now Daisy—"

"Uh-oh. Nothing good ever follows 'now, Daisy.'"

"I'm just saying. I haven't always been rolling in it, but I am now. I know, I know, you told everyone you got out of the divorce okay, but just in case you need some help, just say. Mom and Dad will never know. No one will ever know, I promise—"

"I don't need a thing, sweetie. But you're a love to ask. What's the baby's name going to be?"

"Well, Cameron and I are still fighting about that. Because we three girls got stuck with Camille, Violet and Daisy, you'd better believe there isn't a chance I'm naming this kid after a flower. But Cam, he's got his heart set—he thinks—on Rose. In the meantime, hey, any men on the horizon?''

Daisy's heart instantly leaped to Teague, and in a millisecond flat, her pulse wanted to sing arias. She dropped a dish towel. Then her favorite wooden spoon. ''I'd have to be nuts to get involved with anyone until my life's more settled, don't you think?''

''Well, yeah. But I hate to think of you alone.''

''I'm not afraid to be alone.'' At least that was the whole truth. ''You can be lonelier with the wrong person than being by yourself.''

''You've sure got that right. Been there, done that, didn't like it.''

''What I've been doing...'' In the process of fumbling with the phone, she somehow knocked the napkin holder on the floor. ''Is writing up a résumé. Getting going with my life. Figuring out something serious to do for a career.''

''That sounds good. So what kind of job are you thinking about?''

Daisy knelt down to pick up the scattered bunch of napkins. The truth was, she hadn't thought about sending out résumés, hadn't made any moves to leave White Hills. She hadn't made a single plan since making love with Teague—except for stockpiling every dime she could. Now, though, her throat felt as thick as pea soup, not because she was telling her sister lies, but because they shouldn't have been lies.

''I've been happy to be home for a while,'' she admitted to Violet. ''To be honest, I kind of felt crushed when I got here. It's been good, being back in White Hills, getting back on my feet, but in the long run...you know how restless I am. I was thinking about a job in the travel industry. Cruise director, something like that. Maybe I could be a courier for a jeweler. Or work in insurance in the estates area. There has to be something that a woman who's been spoiled rotten is uniquely qualified to do.''

Her sister laughed.

When Daisy hung up the phone, she found Harry still sitting in his favorite booth—on the same page of the newspaper he'd been before. He shook it, though, as if turning to the next page. ''Sheesh,'' he muttered with a short glance at her, ''whoever you were talking to, don't talk to them again.''

''Why?''

''Because you look like you lost your best friend.''

''No, no. In fact, the call was from my sister. Nothing but great news. She's expecting a baby—'' Daisy motioned to the newspaper. ''When you're done with that, would you mind saving me the classified section?''

''You don't have enough work between me and these projects you're doing with Larson?''

''I'm not looking for jobs, Harry! I just want the lost and found section.''

''What'd you lose?''

Her entire mind, she thought darkly. By one o'clock, though, as she drove Teague's car to his current work site—a den he was paneling in tongue-and-groove redwood for some absentee owners—she'd pepped up.

She found exactly the present she wanted for Teague in the newspaper—although she wouldn't have the chance to see it in person for several days yet. Finding that, though, knowing how badly she wanted to give him this particular gift, forced her to soul search her feelings about Teague.

She was afraid of loving him. She was afraid to trust

her own judgment. And she had reasons for those fears, considering her past history with falling for men who inspired her hormones but never had a chance of working out.

She was mighty afraid a relationship couldn't work out with Teague, either. With reason. But as she found the address and pulled his sacred Golf into the driveway, Daisy told herself that she was armed with several fresh coats of caution. She'd been honest with herself this time. And more than that, so much more than that, Teague was different from any man she'd ever known. This feeling of love was too new, too different, too wonderful to run away from it. She couldn't give it up. She just couldn't. Surely it had a chance to work out if she were just more careful. More smart. More certain that she wasn't repeating past mistakes.

Buoyed with resolve, she hiked up the snowy walk and rapped on the door. There was no decorating to do on this job. Teague just said he'd pay her for helping him finish the wood, because together they could get it done in half the time, and his work schedule was jammed.

Almost before she'd finished knocking on the door, she turned the knob and yelled out an exuberant "Yoohoo!" Teague bounded from a far room to greet her.

That fast, she forgot all her nettling fears. Forgot about being cautious. Forgot all the hard-won lessons she'd learned from picking men who weren't for her.

His grin was more infectious than chicken pox. He galloped down the hall and pounced, taking a kiss as if she were breakfast and he'd been starving for weeks. Then lifted his head and grinned again at her dizzy-eyed response. "Where have you *been?*" he demanded.

"It's ten to one. Didn't you tell me to come at one?"

"Well, yeah. But I've been waiting for you since yesterday." Another kiss, as he stripped off her coat and hat and started pulling her toward the den.

He let her up for air halfway down the hall, only to roll his eyes at her attire. "The slacks, the silky blouse—you call those varnishing clothes?"

"I know they'll get ruined. But they're old. They're what I've got."

"Nah. We'll fix you up better than that."

His theory of fixing her up was to strip her down to the buff, make love with her on the pale-pink carpet of the stranger's hall, and then loan her his shirt to work in. An hour later, give or take, she had a chamois cloth in her hand.

"You need another rag?" he asked her.

"You! Don't come near me! If I need another rag, I'll get it."

"Hey."

"Don't you hey me, *cher*. Every time you come near me, we get diverted for another long while. At this rate, we'll be done with this by February 10 of 2020."

"And this is a problem...how?" He managed to look bewildered at the question she raised, which obviously required her stalking over to his side of the room. She kissed him good. On the navel. The shoulder. Under the chin. And once, swiftly, below the waist.

Then scurried back to her side of the room. "I love making your eyes cross," she mentioned.

"That's because you're an evil, evil woman."

"Don't try complimenting me. You can't get out of making me dinner."

"Somehow I ended up with a really raw deal there. It's your payday but I'm the one doing dinner. How does that work?"

"It works fine in a woman's head, *cher.*"

"Yeah. I get that. What I can't get is how I got bamboozled into the deal to begin with."

It was such nonsense talk. Silliness. She had no idea how three hours passed so fast. He explained the process of finishing the wood. The redwood was all naked and sanded. All she had to do was dip her cloth in the bowl of gunk and "love it in" as he called it.

They'd ambled through conversations. His political views were misguided, but she educated him. She told him stories about growing up in Vermont, the winters, tobogganing and skating with the MacDougal boys next door, her dad leading a Percheron-driven sleigh in the fields with the three sisters trundled up in fifty layers of clothing.

He told her about his mom and dad—how his mom was the blockhead of the family, the one whose genes he'd inherited. "Dad had the patience of a saint, put up with her, put up with me. My sister—Riley—she was the perfect kid. I was the snot."

"You?" Daisy asked in teasing disbelief.

"I know, I know. It's hard to believe. But it seemed like I was always getting suspended for opening my mouth to a teacher. The thing is, when they were wrong, I liked to correct them."

"And you always knew what was right?"

"Yup. I did. And my mom did. Sometimes we butted heads." He thought. "Sometimes we still do, I guess. When she and I go at it, we can generally clear the room faster than a skunk."

"You yell? At your mother?"

"She yells at me. The louder the argument, the more she likes it. My dad used to say, let's hope and pray they broke the mold with you two."

"Did he try giving you two time-outs?"

"Nah. Both my parents were hard-core softies. No discipline. Encouraged Riley and me to explore any damn thing we wanted. Dad even encouraged the arguments, because he said they taught me to think. And Mom—she really screwed me up."

"Yeah?"

"She was the one who pushed the major independence. If I got kicked out of class for speaking my mind, she just laughed. When I fought with Dad to travel around the country my senior summer alone, he thought I was too young. She pushed me to do it. Every damn thing I did wrong, Mom was there to egg me on."

"You're blaming her for the times you got in trouble?"

"Well, I wouldn't put it that way. She just likes to take credit, when sometimes I think I should get some credit myself. But what can you do? She's my mom. I have to let her have her way."

She loved listening. It was so nice, hearing someone talk up their parents. How good they were. That he enjoyed being with them. He told her about Christmases. About hiking the Appalachian Trail. About his history skiing—which involved a lot of drinking at a ski lodge and very little skiing.

He had endless stories to tell—in most of which, he was the villain, or so he claimed. He kept her laughing and talking so much that it only occurred to her later that he'd failed to mention any of the girlfriends in his life. She was about to call him on that when he suddenly walked over, hooked his hands on his hips and shook his head.

"Holy cow, are you *filthy*."

He said it in such an admiring tone that she blinked,

then glanced down. The shirt he'd loaned her was an old blue chambray with a few spots on it. Now it was thoroughly polka dotted with the finishing product and smelled like something that needed fumigating.

She couldn't help it. There was something about working with the wood. Rubbing in the finish. Bringing out the beauty and grain of each board. Loving it in. She'd had no choice about putting her whole self—and his shirt—into it.

Teague shook his head. "Did you play in mud puddles when you were a kid?"

"Are you kidding? I aced the class in sissiness. I got in lots of trouble, but I was always dressed for it."

"You'd never know it now. Come on."

"Come on where? We can't leave. I'm not done." Although, when she glanced out the window, the sun was gone. In fact, the entire day was gone. It was wicked-dark and snowing like a banshee.

"We've been at it nonstop. It's after six. This is nuts. I know you said you didn't have to close up the café tonight. But we both need showers. I need to start dinner, and first off—before the stores close—we have to go buy you some decent clothes."

"Um, Teague." She waved a hand in front of his face to get his attention. "In case you haven't noticed, the one thing in this life I very definitely have is decent clothes. The last thing I need is more."

"You don't have the kind of fancy label stuff I'd buy for you," he insisted.

Oh, God. He dragged her into the General Store on Main Street. It was one of those truly old-fashioned places where you could buy a wedding ring, a hoe, dry powders for headaches and stamps at the same time. The back of the store housed clothes—all on shelves, nothing hung up. The denim was so stiff it could walk by itself. The shirts were so sturdy they were heavier than she was.

"You think these overalls work like a chastity belt?" she asked him. "I don't see how anyone could get in or out of them."

"I hadn't thought about that advantage," he said thoughtfully.

She slugged him. But she couldn't stop him from buying her a new wardrobe of jeans, flannel shirts, gloves, wool socks. "You're sure you can bend your knees in these pants?" she worried.

"You don't wear them *yet,* you silly. First we have to roll up the jeans in dirt and stones, then wash them in bleach. Even then, the fabric will be tougher than the denim you're used to—but the point is, you can spill some paint and varnish and what-all without anything going through the cloth to your skin. And you can wear them over and over, not ruin your pretty stuff."

She gasped when she saw the total. "For Pete's sake, Teague, I can get real clothes for that amount of money."

"Yeah, but would you look this cute? Now. For dinner."

She wasn't aware of being tired, but she'd been up before dawn, cooking and baking, and then really poured on the coals through the hours with Teague. At his house, he started a roaring fire, then parked her on pillows in front of it. "We're going to picnic in here," he told her. "No peeking in the kitchen."

By the time she sank on those pillows, her muscles were creaking, her whole body begging to be let down. It was so different from stress tired, though. She'd loved every minute of the day, loved every minute of being with him.

"Aha," he said finally from the doorway, and came bearing a tray with a lit candle on it.

She twisted into a sitting position and then had to laugh. The candle was set in a crystal holder, very fancy, very nice. The two blue plates matched. The napkins were neatly creased. The wine was served in serious stemware.

The dinner fare was simply peanut butter and bacon sandwiches with chips. "And ice cream bars for dessert—if you finish everything on your plate." He waggled his finger at her. "You don't have to say anything. I'm aware that I'm not exactly a chef at your level."

"Are you kidding? I haven't had this in years."

"It's got all the food groups, right? Or it will as soon as we have the ice cream bars."

"Especially if there's chocolate on the ice cream. You do know that chocolate's one of the critical food groups?"

He looked affronted at the question. "What, you think I was born in a cabbage patch? I never leave chocolate out of a serious meal." He added, "I was missing fruit, but then I figured, there are grapes in the wine."

"Right."

"I guess there's no vitamin D. But tomorrow I could throw you out in the sunshine to take care of that."

"Assuming there is sunshine."

"That is a problem in winter," he conceded. "But assuming we can steal some sunshine, we could have a snowball fight to get our vitamin D."

"I'm amazed how far you're willing to go for the cause of nutrition."

"Hey, there are a lot of things you don't know about me."

They'd been talking and teasing each other all day, yet somehow both of them suddenly stopped talking. The fire snapped and sizzled. Shadows danced on the far walls. Silence seeped between them.

She'd looked at him all day...but not *looked*. He made it so easy to be with him. If he wanted something more from her than time, company, someone to work with—someone to make love with—he never let on. After their exuberant coming together earlier, he hadn't touched her, not in any come-on way, yet desire was like a third heartbeat between them. Just...there. Beating, beating, beating. The sound in her ears. The sound in her heart.

Slowly he pushed aside the dinner tray and held out a hand. She took it, her eyes still on his. She knew the question, although he didn't ask. She gave him the answer, by sweeping her arms around his neck and offering a slow, long, openmouthed kiss.

It seemed like a zillion times that day she'd peeled off her slacks and blouse. This time, though, was different. This time he pushed her blouse up, silky inch by silky inch, his strong callused hands cherishing every touch, every sensation. Yearning, licking hot, sang through her bloodstream. All her life she'd been restless. All her life she'd craved excitement. For the first time she had the crazy idea that he'd been the one she was searching for. Not an event or a place or an activity that was exciting—but him.

Only him.

The thought surfaced, then dissolved. He'd made her clothes disappear, so she concentrated on doing the same magic trick with his. Then they were together again, on their knees, breasts, tummies, pelvises rocking to the same music, creating the same friction, dancing to the same primitive beat.

He lifted his head long enough to smile—one of those all-male disgusting smiles of complete possession. *I own you, babe.*

Well, yeah. He did at that moment. But she owned him right back. Which she showed him at great length and detail.

She woke up past midnight to find him raining kisses all over her face and throat. "Are we waking up for a reason?" she murmured sleepily.

"I wasn't sure if you could sleep here or had to go back to your place. I want you to stay. But you could have to get up awfully early in the morning for the café."

"I do. Five-thirty."

"Well…" More kisses. Concentrating on her cheek-bones. Then her jaw. "I can either get up and drive you home at five in the morning. Or now. Whatever works easiest for you."

She hadn't thought about it, but now that he'd raised the question—and she was awake—she put in a vote. "I don't want to leave you, but it really would be easier to be at my place. Then I just have to walk downstairs to open up. And you don't have to get up at that un-godly hour."

"I don't mind."

"I do. It's not like we can't spend the whole night together another time." She answered his sleepy kisses with more of her own, yet suddenly remembered. "Teague, you don't have to drive me at all. I have your car."

"I know you do. But we're not making love and then you drive yourself home."

He insisted, the silly man. So they dressed and bundled up—she took her new work clothes—and he saw her to the door. Main Street showed no signs of life by then. Occasional crystal snowflakes drifted around the traffic lights. Gossamer-thin clouds whisked around the full moon. The street was theirs, no one else anywhere in sight. A good-night kiss turned into two, then four.

She let him go finally, feeling warm inside all the way to the bones. That *love* word was humming in her pulse again as she unlocked the door and zoomed up the stairs on happy wings. At the top she kicked off her boots, plopped down her packages and bent down to switch on a lamp for light.

Her crazy, giddy smile suddenly faltered.

In the middle of the attic floor—heaven knew how it had gotten there—was a huge, four-foot chocolate heart wrapped in red crinkly paper.

"An early Valentine's Day," the card read. "Four more days until the real thing. This is just the beginning."

The heart was extravagant. Thoughtful. Romantic. Unique. And God knew she loved chocolate.

Yet a shiver chased up her spine.

The present was wonderful, but it was the kind of thing Jean-Luc would have done.

And suddenly she was scared.

Ten

Carrying a dripping spatula, Daisy charged over to the window dividing the kitchen from the café. It wasn't even eight in the morning, yet people were pouring in as if there were no tomorrow.

Her lavender-lemon shortbread cookies were good, but not *this* good.

The café always drew a good morning crowd, but traditionally they were the coffee suckers, the commuters desperate for a fast cup or the retirees gathering for the daily fight about politics. This was…well, everyone. All ages.

"More cookies, Daisy!" Harry bellowed over the transom.

"I'm coming, I'm coming!" Or she was trying to. She hadn't slept well because of worrying about Teague, so she'd come in bleary-eyed—prepared to bake. But damn. Not prepared to need quadruple batches of her shortbread cookies.

She sprinted back to her bowls and oven mitts and cookie sheets, too far to hear what people were saying and too busy to ask Harry what was going on. The shortbread recipe had passed down from her dad's family—the Scots side—but her mom had put the French flair to it, richening it up with the sneaky hints of lavender and lemon. The cookies weren't sweet so much as intense. Addictive. Particularly since she had the best source for the best lavender in the universe— her sister Violet.

A blast of cold air indicated more customers pouring in, and Daisy shook her head. As good as the cookies were—and she knew perfectly well that her skills as a baker made them darn near fabulous—there was still no explaining the high demand in the café this morning.

Harry showed up in the doorway. "I could use you a few more hours, if you want the work. Hell, Daisy, I had no idea you were gonna bring in this many customers when I took you on part-time."

Again she glanced over the transom window. Standing-room only. Every booth was filled. And the door was opening yet again. "For Pete's sake, what on earth are all these people *doing* here?"

"What do we care? They're buying—although I have to admit," Harry wiped his brow, "I'm not used to working this hard. I wish to hell we hadn't let Jason take off for a few days. And Janelle can't do the tables by herself."

"I can see that. But what's the deal? Schools aren't closed today, are they? Or is it some historical person's birthday that I don't remember...?"

Harry rolled his eyes. "Come on, Daisy. You know what they're here for."

She didn't. Not only was she running on half empty, but she'd been too busy to think ever since they opened the café that morning. "I have no idea," she insisted.

"They know all about the heart. The big four-foot chocolate heart. And now they want to know what you're going to do about it—and then what Teague's going to do next." Harry waited for that to sink in before adding, "You didn't think it'd escape anyone in White Hills when UPS brought that package in, did you? The whole town's been watching Teague and you spend time together."

She gulped. All this buzz was about *her?*

Someone called Harry's name and he turned back to the bustling café; she went back to her cookies and baking, pulling out croissants, three loaves of buttermilk-lavender bread, another round of cinnamon clusters, and of course more cookies. But her heart kept sinking.

She'd called Teague last night, sure his feelings would be hurt if she didn't—he'd want to know she'd found the heart. But he must have fallen dead asleep, because he didn't answer. She left a message, trying to express an exuberant thanks and hoping to catch up with him this afternoon. But now...

Unease kept rippling through her. Last night she'd been ruffled by a feeling of déjà vu, and now here was a second déjà vu, even more upsetting and nettling than last night's. She wanted to be thrilled over the heart. What woman wouldn't be charmed by such an extravagant romantic gesture?

Except, last night, her first thought was how many times Jean-Luc had done something like this—tried to pull the wool over her eyes by doing something effusively romantic. For years she'd built up a knee-jerk response. Gift, trick. Get a gift, look over your shoulder for the trick—because something was going to hurt and soon.

She knew that Teague was nothing like Jean-Luc. She knew. And it certainly wasn't Teague's fault that his gift had turned into a spectacle. He couldn't possibly understand how sick and shaken she felt about being the focus of attention. As a kid, God knew, she'd done wild things to get attention, but then she'd married Jean-Luc, the master of public, flashy gestures. So many times Jean-Luc had pulled off some grandiose gift or event in a big public way—as if to show everyone how much he loved her—when they couldn't afford that kind of extravagance. When she'd been working two or more jobs to pay for his last "wonderful" gesture.

Daisy just couldn't seem to stop feeling as if she were floundering. She'd just learned the harsh lesson that when a man felt obligated to shout how much he loved a woman…he likely didn't.

She heard the sheriff's booming voice, glanced out and saw George settling at his usual center seat at the counter—he always had his first cup at the café—only this morning Harry and Janelle were both running to keep up with the other customers. With everyone else so busy, Daisy brought out the pot and a fresh plate of cookies—but she mentally braced. To expect George not to flirt and tease was like wondering if the sun was going to come up in the morning.

Sure enough, George said immediately, "So. I hear you've got yourself a beau."

"Beau? Isn't that a term that died out before the Civil War?"

George just grinned at her attempt to divert him. "So

maybe we need a different term than beau. How about victim? Here you've been in town less than three weeks and already you're breaking hearts."

She was living up to her old reputation, he meant, which stung her conscience even more. She might have been careless with boys back in high school, but she'd grown up. So much so that the idea of hurting Teague in any way bothered her terribly. "Look, George, the heart was a joke. I've been doing some work with Teague, and I let on how much I love chocolate."

"Uh-huh."

"Really, that's all it is!"

"Yeah, well, my ex-wife let on lots of times how much she liked chocolate and I bought her plenty, too. But nothing like a four-foot heart. That had to cost some. And Teague—he's usually the most practical guy in town. Practical, serious, quiet, sticks to himself. For him to make a big gesture like that—oh, baby, you've got him hooked with a capital *H*."

Daisy frowned. The comment made her realize that the townspeople didn't know the real Teague. For darn sure, he was sturdy and strong and practical, but he wasn't all that quiet and didn't naturally have a loner personality at all. He also had a whole personality side that he didn't show easily to others—the side that bought a mutt named Hussy a pink collar. The side that made him lie about his expenses so a wheelchair-bound customer could afford him. The side of him that listened to a down-on-her-luck divorcee—such as herself—and somehow didn't make her feel bad for the failure she'd made of her life. The side that somehow wormed her into telling him the truth, because a woman just knew that she could trust him.

A white-haired lady in a plaid flannel shirt sat down

next to the sheriff, clearly hoping to join the conversation and sniff out more gossip. "Teague did my deck a couple years back. Did a great job, he did. I tried to fix him up with my granddaughter, but he just wouldn't bite, even though she's cute as all can be and smart besides."

"Lorena?"

"Yes, Lorena," she concurred to the sheriff, then turned back to Daisy. "Teague, he said, he'd learned the hard way that marriage wasn't for him. No one could live with him, he said. He'd tried, he said. It's not like he was against marriage, but somehow the woman always ended up mad at him, he—"

"Said," Daisy finished for her. "What can I get for you?"

"Oh, one of those shortbread cookies, dear. When I heard about that big chocolate heart, I almost died..."

Daisy didn't hear the details about how she almost died, because she zipped back in the kitchen for another batch of the cookies. When she returned, the lady in the plaid jacket was still going on as if she'd never left.

"So I said to Sue Ellen, I said, some girl must have hurt him bad. He jokes about being bullheaded and all, but that's not a bad quality in a man. What girl wants a man with no backbone, right, dear? So that can't be the real reason. Some girl had to really stab his heart so bad he was afraid to try again. Or maybe that girl zapped his confidence in the sack, do you think?"

Daisy blinked, opened her mouth, closed it again. She glanced at George, whose mouth was twitching.

"Um," she managed to say.

"Well, whatever she did to him doesn't matter. The point is, he's finally over it if he's chasing after you.

But you'd better snap him up before the rest of the girls realize he's on the market, you know?"

"Thanks for the advice. Would you like coffee with your cookie?"

"Oh, no, dear, I don't drink much coffee, not with my cholesterol." She scooped two more butter-laden cookies on her plate and smiled. "Are you hoping he'll propose?"

"Yeah, Daisy," George echoed, "Are you hoping he'll propose?"

A very rough morning was followed by a rough noon hour, and from there the day went seriously downhill. Around two Daisy started phoning Teague. She wasn't scheduled to work with him that day; he was doing some kind of one-man carpentry work, she didn't remember exactly where. Wherever, he always traveled with his cell phone so customers could always reach him.

Not today. She called at two. Then at two-thirty. Then at three. Then three-thirty. He simply didn't answer and his voice mail didn't activate. He was *always* reachable by phone.

Except for today.

Damnation, where *was* he?

"Teague," the mayor said, "It's not that I have anything personal against your doing this. I just don't think I'm the one you should be asking permission from."

Teague sighed. The mayor, Peter Strunk, had only been in office since November. In the true spirit of Vermont, where nobody really wanted government if they could avoid it, the people had elected a mayor who wasn't likely to interfere in much of anything. The problem with a wishy-washy leader, though, was that he was…well…wishy-washy.

"Look," Teague said, "there's no reason this has to be so complicated. I just want to put up some banners on Main Street for a few hours. Not even a whole day. I'll put them up myself. I'll take them down myself."

"I know, you said all that." Peter had the hen-pecked look he got when he had dinner with his wife. "That's not the issue. I think your idea is charming. I have no objections to it at all. I can't see what harm it would do—"

"So all I need is your permission."

"But the things I'm in charge of—the things a mayor is supposed to do—there's nothing about this kind of thing."

"Mayor," Teague said patiently, "I've asked everyone else. I started with a cop, who sent me to the sheriff. He was gone, but at the office there, somebody said I had to go to the courthouse to get a permit. Then I went to get a permit, but they said they gave permits for things like parades and all, but for an individual request like this, they didn't know. The bottom line is nobody seems to be able to give me a yes but you."

"But I'm not sure…"

Teague stood up. "I know you're not sure." He pulled on his jacket, which he'd never thought he'd have to take off—but who'd have guessed he'd waste almost two hours in the mayor's office? "So the deal seems to be this. Maybe I can't get a 'yes' out of anyone, but no one's given me a 'no' either. So I'm doing it. If somebody uncovers that this is a major felony I'm guilty of, then put me in jail—but don't do it until Saturday, okay?"

"Just hold on, there. I know there have to be safety regulations—"

"I'm sure there are. But I think I'll just go with common sense, rather than waste another whole day trying to figure them out. You have a good day, now, Pete."

Bureaucracy. It was enough to make a man want to move to Alaska. Teague bolted down the courthouse steps and slugged his hands in his pockets against the sharp-shooting wind. Forecast had been for a clear day with no wind. Naturally, it was snowing hard and the wind was fierce as a temper.

He'd missed the whole afternoon's work, but he figured he could make that up by working late tonight. He just had to pick the projects where the owners were gone or on vacation. And although this day had been totally frustrating so far, he glanced at his watch—he still had a good hour of daylight left.

He parked his truck at the far edge of Main Street's business section. Traffic wouldn't quite qualify as rush hour—there was no rush hour in White Hills—but just before dinner, lots of vehicles were cuddled tight at every light, and most of them were crabby. Moms who'd been kid-caring all day, dads who'd just put in nine hours straight, everybody tired of slushy roads and dark evenings. When Teague carted a ladder from the back of his truck, a couple of people honked a hello at him, but no one paid him much attention.

The three main shopping blocks of Main Street were gussied up with old-fashioned gas lights. Before Christmas, the lampposts had been decorated with wreaths and lights, but every season there seemed some excuse to string a banner across the road. It was a challenging job for one man to do alone, particularly when he had to stop traffic now and then to accomplish it. But, hell.

If a guy had to risk breaking his neck for a woman, the woman should at least be worth it, right?

And Daisy, his heart had indelibly told him, was totally worth it.

He knew she had feelings for him...maybe not love yet? So he hadn't won her heart. So they had some problems. But he knew some of her built-in walls now. She had a fear of being ordinary—so obviously he had to find ways to show her that he was never going to treat her as ordinary in a million zillion years. And she had a fear that living in White Hills would doom her to boredom...so he had to find ways to show her that a small town didn't have to be staid.

Suddenly cars started honking. Two pickups stopped. One burly old-timer in a fur cap came barreling out of his truck, looking ready for a fight and furious as all get-out. "What the hell are you trying to do, Teague? Kill yourself?"

"Hey, Shaunessy. No, I'm just having a little trouble—"

"You're having more than a little trouble. You're stopping traffic. You're working on a ladder in a high wind. Now, whatever the hell you're trying to do, let's just get it done so we can all go home."

"Exactly," the bearded man behind him echoed, "what I was thinking."

A couple more townspeople followed up behind him. He'd done work for a lot of them, of course. And although Vermonters could be stubborn and independent, they tended to pitch in when they saw someone in big trouble. It's not as if he would have given up if he'd had to do this totally on his own.

He wasn't giving up. Not on Daisy. Not until he'd tried every last thing he could conceivably think of first.

But it was possible—even probable—that trying to string three sets of banners across Main Street without some help would have taken him all night and then some.

When the townspeople saw what he was doing, he saw a lot of rolled eyes and private grins. But they helped.

Two hours later the job was done.

Then it was just an issue of waiting for Daisy to wake up in the morning and see what he'd done.

The next morning, Daisy rushed over to open the top oven. The smell of char scented the air. An entire tray of croissants was more black-topped than the highway. She pulled out the tray, smacked it on the counter and waved off the smoke in exasperation.

It wasn't as if she'd never had a baking snafu, but it was one thing to have a bad-hair day, another to have two nonstop mean days in a row. And that wasn't even counting bad hair.

Teague was the problem, of course. She tossed down the oven pads. What was going *on?* From the night they'd connected after the blizzard, no day had passed without their talking or being together. But he hadn't called. And she hadn't been able to reach him.

Last night, of course, she'd left town before dinner, driven the back roads to investigate the present she wanted to give him on Valentine's Day. Her heart lifted, just thinking about it—except that worry almost instantly replaced elation. Nothing exactly *had* to be wrong.

But she knew it was. Inside, outside, and every-other-way wrong.

"Daisy!" Harry hollered. "There's another one."

She charged out from the kitchen and found another beaming face at the counter, waiting for her with a little wrapped package, blue and white, with a red bow. "I just brought you a little something, dear!" It was the grandmother with the plaid jacket.

"That's very kind," Daisy said with total bewilderment. In the last hour—since seven that morning—three other people had brought her gifts. She knew all of them, in the way everybody knew each other's faces in White Hills, even if they weren't personal friends. But the first present had been a bar of honeysuckle soap, and the next had been some vanilla sugar scrub.

The grandma in the plaid jacket had wrapped up an oversize loofah. Overall, Daisy was starting to wonder if she was suffering from deodorant fade-out, since all these people suddenly seemed to feel she needed grooming and cleaning products.

"That's so kind of you," she said again. "But you didn't have to give me anything."

"Of course I didn't, dear. But we're all enjoying having you back home in White Hills so much. And your mom and dad and family aren't here right now, so it just seemed like you might need a gift today."

"Today?" Daisy repeated.

The older lady patted her hand. "We all know," she whispered, and then turned around.

Daisy wanted to question her—what exactly did *we* all know?—but the buzzer went off for the bottom oven in the kitchen. She sprinted in, grabbed her hot pads and yanked open the oven door. Her poached apples with vanilla and wine and cardamom and lavender buds simply couldn't fail—yet the pot had bubbled over and made a sizzling mess on the oven floor.

Harry showed up in the doorway. "Phone call for

you in the office. And if this keeps up, I swear I'm dragging my brother in from his vacation. I don't like working this hard. It's against all my principles.''

"I'll help, I'll help, and I promise, I'll get off the phone lickety-split.'' But her heart was soaring higher than an eagle taking flight. The call was surely Teague. Okay, she was anxious and wary and thorny because he'd been so unreachable for the last two days. But as long as he was calling now...well, she wasn't totally appeased yet. But she was sure willing to be.

As she charged into the office, she realized her palms were wet. Realized her thought train: that she was willing to forgive him about anything. Realized that she'd only been separated from him for two days and yet she was wallowing in a palms-wet, can't-sleep, can't-think, constantly anxious state of mind.

She'd never suffered the symptoms before. She'd been wild before, but that seemed her nature. There wasn't much risk in doing something that came naturally to a body. Skydiving and taking off with an artist to another country and that sort of thing had never felt like a risk.

This felt like a risk.

This—God protect her—felt like love.

She grabbed the phone in Harry's office with her heart suddenly galloping at breakneck speed. "Teague?" she said breathlessly.

"It's Dad, Daisy. Not Teague. Who's Teague?"

"Dad." She closed her eyes, took a breath, pinched back the fierce disappointment—and realized all over again that she was in love.

Love was ghastly and terrifying. Who knew? How come her sisters were so happy being in love and loving? This wasn't fun. This was so damn scary she couldn't breathe.

"Daisy, are you there?"

"Yes, Dad. And it's so wonderful to hear your voice. I've really missed you!" That wasn't strictly true at the moment, but Daisy still meant it. She adored her dad. Her two sisters had cleaved more with their mom, but somehow she and Colin always had a special compatibility. When she got in trouble, he'd ream her out—but behind closed doors, he'd laugh with her, as well. He affirmed her spirit, her independence, even when he did the proper-dad-thing and yelled at her when she broke the rules. "Are you and Mom doing okay?"

"Your mom is fine. I'm fine. But I need to get something off my chest."

"Shoot." Daisy saw Harry motioning her to get off the phone, but she sank on the corner of the desk. A woman had priorities. If her dad needed her, that was that.

"Daisy, you told your mother about the divorce. You told your sisters. But you never said one direct word to me."

Guilt bit with sharp teeth. "I never meant to hurt your feelings—"

"If you were having trouble with Jean-Luc, why didn't you say? I know you can handle yourself. I know you wouldn't have gotten a divorce unless the situation had become hell for you. But I thought we could always talk. I never met anyone who got so old they couldn't use support from family. Why haven't you called?"

"I'm sorry." She took a breath, knowing she'd been avoiding her dad. "I know we're overdue a heart-to-heart." She thought she'd conquered a lot of her pride, partly because of finding Teague. Talking with him.

Somehow telling him things she'd never have told anyone else. But there was a level of pride she still had trouble dipping beneath. That asking-for-help thing. That admitting when she was wrong. That admitting when she was scared.

"You're doing all right now?"

"Fine," she told him, and then grappled for more honesty. "Well…not fine. Because a man entered the picture who I really care about. I wasn't looking. And I hadn't planned on looking until I had money, a job, my whole life back together. But now is when I found him."

"You love this guy?" her dad asked gruffly.

So easily, so strongly she said, "Yes." But she closed her eyes and added, "Dad, there was a reason I didn't tell you anything before. Everyone in the family's done so well with their lives—in spite of some terrible things happening, like with Camille losing her first husband, and Violet believing for so long she couldn't have a baby. I seemed to be the only one who really bungled things."

"You didn't bung—"

"Yeah, I did. And I didn't want to be a disappointment to you."

"You couldn't disappoint me, you goose." Her dad talked a few more minutes about family business. How her mom had managed to plant a garden in spite of the heat. How Camille was loving being a stepmom to her hellion teenage twins and talking about starting up an animal shelter. How Violet couldn't talk about anything else but how wonderful the pregnancy was.

When Daisy hung up, she was smiling. Smoke was billowing out of the oven; Harry was exasperated with her, and no one was waiting on the impatient customers at the counter. But as she dashed out to help, she felt so, so, so much better for having talked with her dad.

She *did* need to put her life back together, not go into any relationship as a dependent. But even with the fear she'd built up about repeating her bad judgment with men—she *knew* Teague was different. Knew his heart was honest, his ethics straight and true, his capacity for love generous and huge.

Yet as she charged into the restaurant to help put out fires—the table of seven near the far window looked downright furious at how long they'd been waiting— she suddenly stopped dead. That particular far window looked out on Main Street. The east side of Main Street. The side that led to the shops and main business district.

Maybe she'd glanced out the window earlier, maybe not—there wasn't much to see in those pitch-black hours before sunrise. But the watery sun had poked over the horizon now. She immediately saw the banners— all three of them.

HAPPY
BIRTHDAY
DAISY!

Loopy daisies and black-eyed Susans hung from both sides of the banners, climbing up the lampposts. And when she saw the banners, suddenly all sound seemed to stop in the café. Even the impatient family of seven was grinning. Staring at her.

Now she got it—all the customers this morning.

All the presents.

Only it wasn't her birthday or even close.

For an instant she couldn't move or breathe. It was another charming, impulsive gesture. Romantic. Gran-

diose. Exactly what had given her an uneasy stroke
when he'd given her the four-foot heart. And since this
was bigger and even more public, she probably should
be having a stroke times two.

Instead she sucked in a breath, took care of the impatient customers, and the instant she got a free second,
she ran into Harry's office to use his private phone.

No surprise, Teague didn't answer—either his home
phone or his cell. But this time she left a firm message.
"This is Daisy. Either call me or I'm going to strangle
you with my bare hands. And that's a promise."

Eleven

Teague pulled over to the side of the road, braked and rolled down the window. The blast of cold air wasn't enough to wake him up, so he slapped his cheeks.

He *had* to get some sleep. He'd been burning the candle at both ends all week—and all for a good cause. He just had one more project to pull off before he could crash. It wouldn't wait because tomorrow was Valentine's Day.

As whipped as he was, his mood was still elated. This would get her, he thought. It was the Valentine's present of all Valentine's presents. All right. So it wasn't exactly romantic in the classic sense, but romantic was what showed love, right?

It's not like it was an appliance.

This was big. No one could call it ordinary. It was nothing like that lazy son of a gun would have given her—something she had to give back, something she really had no use for. Daisy already had zillions of jewels and crap like that. She was suspicious of that kind of thing. He'd had to find something that would really, really be a surprise for her—and it damn well wasn't easy to surprise a woman who'd lived a lot higher than Teague ever dreamed of.

He put the truck in gear and plodded in, turning into the massive parking lot just before four. Barbara Vanhorn was waiting for him. She came on to anything in pants, wore her hair all moussed up, wore tight skirts to show off her legs. And she was a born saleswoman. Still she was okay to deal with.

"Teague, I was afraid you were a no-show."

"Didn't mean to be late. Just been running a few minutes behind all day. You got the paperwork on my baby?"

"Of course. Come on into the office." She sashayed into her cubicle. Steel-blue chairs, steel-blue desk, nothing there but the usual forms. "I could have done better for you."

"I know you could have."

"It's just…not the right toy for you, you know? You need something sexier. Classier. You could have blown me over with a feather when you said you want this."

Teague suspected that sexy and classy started and ended her vocab on adjectives. At least when talking about her favorite subject. "This is what I want," he said.

"And you've got it, hon. You just call me anytime."

"Good." It took a few minutes to fill out the fifty thousand forms. "I need this delivered first thing in the morning—like by eight. To the Marble Bridge Café. To Daisy Campbell. And under no circumstances are you to tell her who it's from."

"We settled all this yesterday. Stop worrying," Barb said.

"I mean it. I'm holding you to your promise. I want to tell her myself, but I just want to do it my own way."

"Hey, where's your trust? You *know* me. I think this whole surprise is just darling," she assured him.

When he stood up, he had the sixth sense she was going to wrap her arms around him and claim a big hug—for old-time's sake, and for the sake of the sale, and for the sake of it being a nice day. And any other old sake Barb could think up.

She was nice enough, but right then he didn't seem to want any boobs pushing against his chest but one woman's.

In fact, right then he didn't want to be kissed, hugged or flirted with by anyone except Daisy.

But, man, he was risking everything he had—everything he was—and he knew it. Valentine's Day didn't have to be the crunch, but a crunch was imminent. Once Daisy had enough money to take off, that was still her plan—unless a better plan surfaced damn fast.

He was hoping she'd think he was a better plan.

When he climbed back in the truck, he damn near forgot to shut the door—he was that exhausted. He got home. He knew he got home, because he heard the phone ringing. And ringing. And ringing. He seemed to have made it to the bed, seemed to still have his boots on, didn't care about the boots or the phone.

He suspected it was Daisy. She'd left messages before. Increasingly annoyed messages.

He just couldn't get it all done—his work, the surprises. Not and pull it all together before Valentine's Day. Besides which, he was a coward. Unless he could prove to Daisy that life in White Hills—life with him—

wasn't going to be ordinary or dull, a life where she could get back that pride in herself she'd lost with the French Creep…he knew he was going to lose her. He couldn't accept that. And for damn sure he couldn't face it until he had to.

So he let the phone ring. In fact, by that time, he didn't even open an eye. In his mind he heard her talking to him. These last few days he'd fiercely missed working with her. Missed sleeping with her. Missed talking with her. Missed her hoity-toity clothes and the way she arched her right eyebrow when she was teasing him. He missed the way she walked. He missed the shape of her mouth.

Even from the depth of sleep, Teague seemed to be replaying the obvious—not the obvious dream but the totally obvious truth.

He couldn't imagine living without her.

Daisy answered her cell phone only because someone rang three times already—which meant that someone obviously couldn't take a hint. She was *busy*. "What?" she spit into the receiver.

"Daisy! You've got to come down to the restaurant right now!"

"Come on, Harry. This is the first day I asked to have off. Jason's back. You don't need m—"

"It's not that. I don't need you to work. I just need you to come down. Now. Fast."

She had her hands absolutely full with Teague's present, but to appease Harry—who after all, had been good to her—she shoved on shoes and sprinted downstairs.

She saw the crowd gathered at the front door, not a crowd in line for the restaurant but a crowd facing the stairs to the apartment, so her immediate thought was uh-oh. When she reached the bottom of the steps, she counted heads. Not every single body in White Hills was sardined into the restaurant lobby, but it had to be close. Faces stared at her, wearing expectant expressions. Nosy expressions. Strangely worried expressions.

Daisy didn't need any internal conscience warning her uh-oh this time. She spun around to escape back upstairs—fast—and she would have made it, if Harry hadn't lumbered through the crowd and grabbed her hand. She assumed the point of all this lunacy was for her to see something in the restaurant, but instead of tugging her inside, Harry tugged her outside.

She was wearing navy wool slacks and a Valentine-red sweater, respectable inside clothes, but naturally no coat or jacket. The wind blistered her ears before she'd taken the first step. A woman was waiting at the curb, wearing a skirt short enough to risk her rear end getting frostbite, a showy smile on her face. To her right were two townspeople holding cameras. The local newspaper—a weekly—had a snot-nosed kid holding a businesslike camera on her left. Obviously everyone was counting on her to react in some spectacle-like way, but for an instant Daisy couldn't pin down what on earth she was supposed to react to.

Then she got it. Or kind of. Behind the lady with the showy smile was…well, she had to squint to identify what it was. A vehicle, for sure. But not exactly a car or a truck or an SUV.

And then she remembered. It was one of those things the guys took to war. A Hummer. A used Hummer—truth to tell, it looked like a reinforced used Hummer—painted daisy yellow with a big red Valentine's Day bow tied prettily on the steering wheel.

Daisy closed her eyes tightly for a good long millisecond, thinking *no,* this couldn't be happening. She thought she'd loved him. She actually thought she'd loved him. But this…

This was the end of the line for Teague.

Teague knew he was dreaming. On the other side of his closed eyelids, there seemed to be bright light—which couldn't be, since he'd stumbled into bed just a few minutes ago in the pitch-black. But he figured the bright light was symbolic. Dreams were goofy like that. And the only time he dreamed at all was when he was so wasted tired that he couldn't make sense of anything, anyway.

Still, this dream was different. Powerful. Gripping. Whether it was symbolic or wishful thinking or plain old need, Daisy was there. He heard her whispering, "Teague? Teague!" in that exotic, sexy voice of hers. And her perfume wafted around him, the scent that always shot testosterone straight to his brain.

He wasn't completely surprised that Daisy was there, of course. He knew the Hummer'd do it.

The heart—he'd definitely wanted to give her the heart, but bottom line, giving your best girl chocolate on Valentine's Day wasn't exactly a headline-news idea. He needed the opposite of ordinary. He thought the birthday banners on Main Street was a better idea—partly because he couldn't believe her Jean-Luc would have done such a thing. Also the rest of the town would get off on it, he knew, so that Daisy'd be exposed again to how honestly nice people were in White Hills. It *was* nice to live in a place where people knew you, paid attention, watched out for you. It wasn't skinny-dipping in the Riviera, no. But they could do that kind of junk on vacations if she wanted. Daisy knew what it was like to live with strangers and no one she could count on. He couldn't believe that would be her first choice ever again.

He'd heard feedback that the banner thing had gone over big—which was good—but Teague had known up-front that wasn't enough. He'd needed to come up with something to really give her a jolt. Dais had to be close to saving enough for a car down payment by now—had to be close to leaving. So the Hummer…well, it was a long way from the cool sports cars she'd likely driven in France, but the thing was, he'd driven with her. She needed to be surrounded by steel. She didn't need cute; she needed a vehicle that could get itself out of ditches, that could go uphill when nothing else could go uphill. He fully realized that Daisy wasn't worried about issues like that. It was his problem, that she drove like a bat out of hell.

Her issue, though, was that she wasn't an exotic flower. He knew she wanted to be—that she'd always wanted to be. But the truth was, his Daisy was no-nonsense to the bone. She loved working. Real work. She loved making something out of nothing, loved feeling challenged, loved getting her hands all messy in stains and varnishes, loved cooking herself rather than being waited on.

Teague couldn't imagine telling her that her self-image was goofy, that her dreams didn't fit her at all. But he thought, really thought, that the Hummer was perfect for her. She could go anywhere in blizzards or storms. Carry tools or wedding cakes. Daisy, being a doer in every way, didn't need a sports car that required constant attention, but a vehicle that enabled her to take off on any wild ambition she had.

Besides which, a Hummer *so* wasn't ordinary.

He smiled in the dream. Hell, it was hard not feeling high as the sky. When he'd gone to bed, his whole world looked precarious, the fear of loss hanging over his heart like a lead pendulum...but now everything was coming right.

Daisy'd quit talking. The warm body snuggled next to him made him smile all over again. He could feel her slow, soft tongue. Licking his cheek. Then his nose. Then his mouth.

She was hot for him. Really hot. It seemed like all his life he'd been dreaming about her warm, lithe body, about her warm, wet, lithe tongue. Almost like this. Not exactly like this, but almost.

Suddenly the "almost" part of the dream struck him as a tad disturbing. Because a cold, wet nose suddenly nuzzled his cheek.

And Daisy sure as hell didn't have a cold, wet nose.

His eyelids shot wide-open. The daylight pouring in the windows almost blinded him. From somewhere he could smell fresh coffee. And the affectionate female body lying in bed with him wasn't Daisy, but a dog. A young, scruffy mutt with black-and-white fur and brown eyes and no heritage to brag about—or several heritages to brag about, depending on one's point of view. The instant she discovered he was awake, her long, feathery tail started thumping at several thousand miles an hour. Someone had put a bushel basket next to his bed, filled to overflowing. Teague saw a powder-blue collar, a powder-blue leash, balls, pull toys, carpet cleaning products, kibble, and...he squinted...a powder-blue bowl with HUSSY II engraved on it.

"What the hell?" Teague muttered groggily, which made the puppy respond with ecstatic enthusiasm, leaping on him to lavish his entire face with kisses. "Aren't you a darling? But whoa, baby, take it easy, take it easy..."

Only one person in the universe would have given him a pup named Hussy, and he promptly forgot the dog—because his real-life hussy was suddenly standing in the doorway.

Some guys fantasized about a woman in corsets and black lace. His fantasy woman was dressed in overalls, no shoes, thick floppy socks, and her thick, elegant hair looked determined to escape a ponytail. He couldn't speak for a second, because she was so darn beautiful she stole his breath. When it came down to it, she was so beautiful she was probably always going to steal his breath. Today, though, it was more than those gorgeous bones and lush mouth and exotic, sexy eyes. It was the vulnerability in her expression, the anxiety she couldn't quite hide—although God knew, she tried.

"You're in trouble up to your eyebrows, Larson," she said sternly.

"I'm in trouble? *I'm* in trouble?! What is this dog?!"

"Your birthday present."

"It's not my birthday until October."

She cocked a foot forward. "This is relevant to what? You put up those giant Happy Birthday banners for me all over Main Street, and my birthday isn't until August."

"What day?"

"The thirty-first." Her eyes narrowed. "Don't distract me. You're going to take that car back."

"The hell I am," he said amiably. "Just for the record, is the dog house-trained?"

"They said she was, at the rescue place, but..." When Daisy opened the balcony door, the pup leaped down from the bed and galloped outside, only falling over its feet once. "My take is that she's well people-trained. If you let her outside every ten minutes, she doesn't go in the house." With the pup safely in the fenced yard, Daisy turned back to him and started up her rant again. "Nobody gives me a car, Teague. I don't want to owe anyone, ever again. You know I'm not rolling in money, but I've saved almost every dime since coming home. I can do without until I've got it together. I don't need charity."

"Well, of course you don't. But I figured you knew I was nothing like Jean-Luc. You would never worry that I was trying to buy your affection or trying to con you. Right?"

"Well, of course that's right, but—"

God, it felt good, hearing her say it. So he forged on, "So I knew you'd understand this was completely different. I'd never do anything to undermine that fierce pride of yours. I just honestly thought you'd need your own car if we were married."

That vulnerable expression intensified times ten. She sucked in a breath, and then, as if she still couldn't get enough oxygen, sank on the far edge of the bed.

"You don't want to get married, remember? You can't seem to work with other people, you said. You'd given up on relationships, you said. It's not that you wanted to be alone, but you figured you were too ornery for anyone to survive living with you, you—"

"Yeah, I know what I said." He crooked his finger, urging her to come closer. "But didn't you notice the strangest thing happening? That we were working together? Really well?"

"Well, I wouldn't say *really* well. I bossed you around that one day in front of your customer—"

"You did. And I was astounded how much I liked

that.'' He crooked his finger at her again, since she still hadn't budged from the foot of the bed. ''Who would have guessed it could be so much fun to work with someone else? Since I'm as mean as I always was, I realized the difference had to be you. You were the one who made it fun. And I figured if you could work with someone as pigheaded as me, marriage would be a piece of cake. You'd like it. We could have sex a couple of times every day. And we could eat together and work together and fight together. I could teach you to run a planer and a band saw. You could take me to a nude beach on the Riviera once a year. We could have kids. Have all our families together at Christmas. We could add and subtract from that general list, but doesn't it sound like a good basic plan?''

His Daisy didn't cry. Ever. But suddenly her eyes welled up and were glittering like crystals, making him pretty sure—not positive, but pretty sure—she thought it was a good basic plan. He started breathing again. His heart was still scared, but not as gut-scared, soul-scared, aching-scared as it had been the night before.

''But what about all those things you said, Teague—''

''We already talked about those. So how about if we talk about all the things *you* said?'' Since she seemed to be frozen in place, he sat up, reached over and tugged her over the comforter to his side. And when she was there, on his down pillow, all tangled up in sheets and comforter, he pinned her down, first by kissing her left temple, then her left ear, then her left cheek…very, very tenderly. ''You said White Hills made you feel stifled.''

''That used to be true,'' she affirmed.

''So, just for the record, if it's still true, I don't give a damn if we live in Timbuktu.''

"I think right here in White Hills might just be perfect," she said, and then closed her eyes, when he finished kissing the whole right side of her face and then
honed in on her mouth. He had to linger over that kiss,
because it wasn't funny, how afraid he'd been that he
might never hold her again, that she would leave him,
that it was an impossible dream that she could ever love
him.

"You're not bored here?"

"I haven't had a second to be bored." Her fingertips
traced his jawline, and although he knew he was out of
his mind with hope, he could swear he saw both lust
and wonder in her eyes. "You know what? I used to
think that the place you lived mattered. But the place
isn't the source of excitement. You are, Larson."

"Me? I'm as ordinary as they come. And that's an
honest problem, I realize. You're exotic and rare and an
orchid in every way. When I'm doomed to be nobody
fancy."

"Teague?"

"What?"

"I have a secret to tell you." She motioned him just
a little closer, which was a trick. When he obediently
moved to accommodate her, she twisted until she was
on top, and then exercised some kissing techniques of
her own. She probably thought she had him pinned,
which was certainly an illusion he wanted her to have,
because he loved Daisy at her most dangerous. She
kissed him and kept kissing him. Ardently. Winsomely.
Sweetly. "You love me," she told him.

"You think that's a secret? Hell, I've known that for
ages." He started unhooking the overalls. "I adore you,
Dais. I love your fancy side and your practical side.
Your elegance and your common sense. Your spirit.

Your pride. Your heart—and I promise, I'll spend a lifetime protecting that wonderful, giving, precious heart of yours."

"Can I tell you another secret?"

"We have to keep talking?"

"Just for a little longer," she promised him. "I just wanted to tell you...I love you. I never thought I'd find a man I could be honest with. A man I could trust. A man who didn't want a woman to walk in his shadow. I always thought I had to hide who I really was."

He cut her off, not because he didn't want to talk to her for the next hundred years. But because she'd hit him where it counted.

She knew him. Really knew him. Knew about his dog, knew about his faults and weaknesses, knew things about him no one else did—and still loved him. It was what he wanted to give her for a lifetime, that total trust that she could be herself with him, that she was safe, that they'd protect each other through life's challenges.

Right then, though, he'd just as soon she didn't think he was *totally* safe. She could cope with a little danger. She liked a little risk. And as soon as he got the rest of her clothes off, he felt inspired to give her all the danger and risk she could handle—along with that other wild four-letter word. Love.

Epilogue

Daisy tiptoed upstairs, where her sister's baby was sleeping in the old nursery. She found Rose awake. Not wide awake, but awake enough that she was surely justified in picking her up.

She crooned softly as she carried her niece over to the window overlooking the backyard. ''I finally got you alone, didn't I, little one? How are you ever going to know that I'm your favorite aunt if everyone else always grabs you? But I've got you now, you darling…''

Below, the family party was in full swing. Daisy gave herself full credit for the reunion—it was her birthday today, August 31—but the day was just an excuse. As close as their family was emotionally, it had been years since they'd had a chance to really spend time together—much less at the Campbell family homestead.

Below, Cameron and Pete, her brothers-in-law, were

both holding spatulas in front of a flaming barbecue and
looking bewildered. Pete's two teenage boys had gotten
ahold of a hose, and were racing around, soaked to the
bone. God knew how many dogs were chasing them.
Hussy II fit right in with Camille's pack, but Daisy only
recognized the shepherd and the bloodhound—the rest
looked like the derelict rescue dogs they all were. Violet's cats were supervising the party from the cool, safe
height of the shade trees.

Her gaze softened as she spotted her parents. Margaux was carrying another bowl outside—two picnic
tables were set up and already sagging with food, a
good thing since nothing coming off the grill had a
prayer of being edible. Colin stepped up behind Margaux and swung her in a hug. The two looked at each
other the same way they always had when they thought
their three daughters didn't notice. Even after all these
years, the love between them glowed like sunshine, silent, warm, healing.

"You know Grandma and Grandpa, don't you,
Rose," Daisy murmured. "Grandma always smells like
lavender. And when you get a little older, she'll let you
make cookies and all kinds of messes in the kitchen.
And then Grandpa...oh, you're going to love Grandpa.
You get just a little bigger, and he'll swing you up in
the air and tickle you and make you laugh..."

She heard a footstep behind her and half turned.

"I wondered where you'd disappeared to—but it
wasn't too hard to guess," Teague said wryly.

Not that she was prejudiced, but her husband was the
handsomest of all the men there, so tall and lean, so
full of hell with those dark eyes and sexy smile. She
smiled when he bent down to kiss her. "You surviving
my family okay?"

"They're terrific."

"You were worried?"

"How could I not be worried? I had visions of three more women just like you and the kind of father who thinks no man is ever good enough for his daughter."

"Ha. My dad took one look at you and said I'd *finally* developed some judgment in men." She added wryly, "Which was true. I'm keeping you, Mr. Larson, and that's that."

"Yeah, well, I'm keeping you, Mrs. Larson, and that's *that*."

She grinned, until the baby suddenly let out a small squall, as if offended to be ignored for so long. "You want to hold your niece?" she asked Teague.

"Not exactly. They're pretty scary when they're that little. Um…"

She didn't give him a choice, simply lifted the baby into Teague's arms. He looked alarmed for several seconds, but then Teague was complete mush in the heart area—which she knew. His arms instinctively snuggled the baby. Rose opened her eyes and blew a bubble for her uncle.

"I'm in love," Teague admitted gruffly. "She's scary, mind you. But if ours is even half this beautiful, I'll be okay. I think. Possibly. Maybe."

"Ours?" Daisy repeated.

His gaze shot to hers. "Did you think I wouldn't guess?"

"I'm not sure yet," she whispered. "I haven't had the test. Haven't been to a doctor."

"I'm sure. And I couldn't be happier, lover. A little scared, I admit it. But I can't think of anything I want in this life more than a baby with you." Again he leaned down to kiss her, this time a kiss of lingering tenderness that made her heart sing.

A clatter of footsteps running up the stairs interrupted them. "Hey, you two. Enough of the mush. My God, every time you turn around, someone's kissing in this family," Camille complained. She was out of breath, just from climbing the stairs, but then she was already big as a tugboat and the baby wasn't due for two more months. She waggled her fingers. "Hand over my niece."

"She doesn't want you," Daisy told her. "She wants her favorite aunt. The one who's going to give her drums and cymbals and lots of noisy toys, right, pumpkin?"

"If you don't let me have a turn, Mom'll be up here, and you all know no one can get a baby out of her hands."

"You've all had more time with Rose than I have," Daisy argued.

"But I'm going to have the next one, so I need the baby-holding experience. Besides. I'm the youngest. And you two always let me have my own way, so I don't think you should start making exceptions now."

"Of all the sissy, weak-kneed arguments," Daisy began, but Violet interrupted.

"You two are going to make me cry. How many years has it been since we had a chance to bicker like this?"

They started laughing, even if their laughter turned just a little misty-eyed in the process...but then the baby let out a single soft wail. All three of them naturally quietened down as Violet took Rose to the rocker and started nursing her.

"She's so beautiful, Vi," Daisy said softly.

"I know, I know. I feel so lucky."

"We're all lucky. Five years ago we all seemed in so much trouble that I wasn't sure if any of us could find our way."

Camille put a hand on her stomach. "Through thick and thin, I always knew you two would be there for me. And now I think back and realize how much we learned about love—real love, tough love, the kind of love that really lasts—from Mom and Dad."

"Yeah, so did I," Violet agreed. "I didn't see it at the time. Not until I met Cameron. But knowing the kind of love that really makes a difference—it started with all of us."

Daisy found herself sitting on the windowsill, a smile on her face that refused to go away. It was so wonderful, to have her sisters and family together again. To see how Camille and Violet had moved on from such devastating blows to create stronger, better lives for themselves. To see them both so fiercely in love.

Her, too, she mused. She wasn't sure when Teague had disappeared, but knowing him, she could have guessed he'd give her some alone time with her sisters. Her gaze drifted to the yard below, where Teague was walking with her parents in the original lavender garden that Margaux had started as a young bride.

As if sensing her love, Teague looked up. He didn't interrupt his conversation with her parents…just looked at her.

And she just looked back. Her heart welled up with so much love she could hardly stand it. She loved that man—and she loved seeing him with her family.

They were all home. It didn't get better than this.

* * * * *

**introduces an exciting new family saga
with**

DYNASTIES: THE DANFORTHS

**A family of prominence...
tested by scandal, sustained by passion!**

COMING NEXT MONTH

#1627 ENTANGLED—Eileen Wilks
Dynasties: The Ashtons
Years ago, Cole Ashton and Dixie McCord's passionate affair had ended when Cole's struggling business had taken priority over Dixie. Now, she was back in his life and Cole hoped for a second chance. But even if he could win Dixie once more, would Cole be able to make the right choice this time?

#1628 HER PASSIONATE PLAN B—Dixie Browning
Divas Who Dish
Spunky nurse Daisy Hunter never thought she'd find the man of her dreams while on the job! But when a patient's relative, athlete Kell McGee, arrived in town, she suddenly had to make a difficult decision—stick to her old agenda for finding a man or switch to passionate Plan B!

#1629 THE FIERCE AND TENDER SHEIKH—Alexandra Sellers
Sons of the Desert
Sheikh Sharif found long-lost Princess Shakira fifteen years after she'd escaped her family's assassination. As the beautiful princess helped heal her homeland, Sharif passionately worked on mending Shakira's spirit. Though years as a refugee had left her hardened, could the fierce and tender sheikh provide the heat needed to melt Shakira's cool facade and expose her heart?

#1630 BETWEEN MIDNIGHT AND MORNING—Cindy Gerard
When veterinarian Alison Samuels moved into middle-of-nowhere Montana, she hardly expected to start a fiery affair, especially with hunky young rancher John Tyler. To J.T., this tantalizing older woman was a stimulating challenge and Alison was more than game. But J.T. hid a dark past and Alison wasn't one for surprises....

#1631 IN FORBIDDEN TERRITORY—Shawna Delacorte
Playboy Tyler Farrel was totally taken when he laid eyes on the breathtakingly beautiful Angie Coleman. She was all grown up! Despite their mutual attraction, Ty wouldn't risk seducing his best friend's kid sister until Angie, sick of being overprotected, decided to step into forbidden territory.

#1632 BUSINESS AFFAIRS—Shirley Rogers
When Jenn Cardon placed the highest bid at a bachelor auction, she had no idea she'd just landed a romantic getaway with sexy blue-eyed CEO Alex Dunnigan—her boss! Thanks to cozy quarters, sexual tension turned into unbridled passion. Alex wasn't into commitment but Jenn had a secret that could keep him around...forever.

SDCNM1204